Laralynn's TURN

An Evergreen Novel

Joann Herley

ACKNOWLEDGEMENTS

Cover Photos by:
© Tatyana Ivanikova | Dreamstime.com
Edited by: EBH and P. Maier
Formatted by: P. Maier

Dedication

Teresa Henderson

My Lovely Courageous Friend

Special Thanks

Thank you to my husband for his unending love and encouragement.

Thank you to Jen Miller for her daily notes that encouraged me to keep writing this story, brightened my day with humor, and offered me her friendship.

Thank you to P. Maier for always reading the rough copy and making it look beautiful. I couldn't have done this without you.

Thank you to J. D. Myers for your comments and suggestions.

Thank you to those of you that have read all my books. I have loved every note and comment you have sent me, and it has made my journey more meaningful.

Thank you to the new readers that have taken a chance on this book.

Other Books from the Author

The Evergreen Series

Seized by Obscurity
Escaping Obscurity
Protected From Obscurity
Shattering Obscurity

Evergreen Novels and Novellas

Trapped ALONE
Laralynn's TURN

Coming Late Summer of 2017

Revenge – ON POISON WINGS

List of Characters

Evergreen Castle

Laralynn - Human and Daughter of Lara and Thomas
Lara - Vampire and Lady Evergreen
Thomas - Vampire and Lord Evergreen
Baxter - Vampire and Evergreen Army
Oliver - Vampire and Evergreen Army
Meadow - White Witch of Evergreen Castle
Preston - Commander of the Evergreen Army
Gavenia - Hawk Shifter and Mate to Tate
Tate - Vampire, Brother to Thomas and Mate to Gavenia
Elda - Vampire and Evergreen Army

Black Thistle Castle

Gautier - Warlock and Lord of Black Thistle
Kayleigh - Wolf Shifter and Lady of Black Thistle
Killian - Wolf Shifter and Guardian to Lady Kayleigh
Alicia - Wolf Shifter and Mate to Killian
Gustavo - Vampire and Commander of the Black Thistle Army
Desirae - White Witch of Black Thistle Castle
Rex - Head of the Black Thistle Council

Withering Rose

Jario - Vampire and Traitor to Evergreen Castle (Sir Quinsley)
Ewan - Swan Shifter

Primrose Pond

Aslev - Human and Sister to Astra
(Previously known as Velsa - Black Magic Witch
before her powers and magic were taken from her)
Astra - White Witch and Sister to Aslev

Firelight Castle

Violeta - Mistress of Firelight Castle and Swan Shifter
Angus - Protector of Firelight Castle and Wizard
Francey - Human and Lady in Waiting to Mistress Violeta

Woods Village

Bertha - Tavern Owner
Jingles - Wagon Driver
Balgair - Vampire known as the Silver Fox and Power Collector

Alabaster

Nora - Queen of Alabaster and Lioness Shifter
Teppo - King of Alabaster and Lion Shifter
Topaz - Healer of Alabaster
Ruby - Healer of Alabaster
Crew - Brother to Teppo and Lion Shifter
Vitas - Commander of the Army, King's Regent, and Lion Shifter

Prologue

Laralynn sat leaning against the rocks that overlooked Wispet Canyon. She remembered the way it used to look with its blackened stone walls, dry stream beds, and crumbling stone cottages. The Wispets had been driven from their beloved canyon, and every living thing had perished. Black Magic had swirled within the canyon walls and eagerly claimed the gifts from any vampire that had been brave enough to enter. Its destruction had been caused by the curse of an angry, jealous witch, and it had stood this way for over a hundred years.

Since that dark time, the curse on the canyon had finally been broken. The Wispet Queen had returned, and once again, her Wispets had filled the canyon with rows of fragrant lavender, pink flowering trees, and crystal clear streams. The view offered a feeling of peace to anyone that gazed upon it.

On this day, the beautiful canyon had little to offer her, for Laralynn's mind was deeply troubled. She had discovered closing her eyes to sleep brought nightmares of the past instead of sweet dreams to help her rest. For months, her dreams had been filled with scenes of Magna's heart being ripped from her body by an old woman, her mother's death, or seeing the memories and magic being torn from Velsa's mind. They were all events she had witnessed, and she had finally figured out a way to make them stop. She had confronted them with a magical sword she created in her dream, and they had crept back into the shadows allowing her to sleep peacefully.

Unfortunately, her peaceful sleep was short-lived, for now, a faceless man had begun to haunt her dreams. He was coming for her magical sword, and he would stop at nothing to make it his own.

"Who is this faceless man that invades my dreams, Starlight?" she asked, as she felt her mare's nose nudge her cheek. "Has he only been created by my imagination, or is this a premonition? Does he mean to do harm to Evergreen or me? I fear the worst, Starlight. I fear something terrible is coming."

Chapter 1

A Distant Light

The sun had finally set, and Jario eagerly scanned the bright orange horizon for any sign of land. Since his narrow escape from Black Thistle Castle, he had spent too many days at sea hidden within the dark bowels of the *Withering Rose*, and he was ready to rid himself of its foul-smelling crew. To survive, he had succumbed to the humiliation of gathering scraps from the captain's table and drinking the blood from rats that had carelessly made their way onboard. His stomach yearned for a tankard of ale and a bowl of hot rabbit stew. It had been hard enough to stay invisible using his gift of haze, but to go without the taste of human blood had been his near undoing.

As he moved toward the ship's bow, he noticed a strange dark shadow against the darkening sky. A silhouette of what he thought were towers reached far above an expanse of trees. A pale violet light from the tallest tower caught his eye, and he stared as it flickered in the darkness.

"There it is," shouted one of the crew. "See the towers against the horizon."

Not wanting to listen further, Jario climbed onto the railings and dove into the dark water. He was well beyond the *Withering Rose* when he surfaced and could not hear the warnings of the ship's crew as he swam toward the island's shore.

"They say it is a witch's castle surrounded by fire," replied the man standing next to the railing.

"Come away from the railings. If you stare at the light in the tower, the witch will draw you near," warned another man as he turned his head away from the tower's light. "Heed my warning; the Isle of Flames burns bright with the souls of many a curious man."

* * *

The moment Jario reached the island's shore, he felt an unexpected warmth surrounding him. As he stood and stepped from the foam of a retreating wave, he felt heat seeping through the soles of his boots. Other than the few times he had found himself stranded in the sunlight, he had not felt anything close to this sensation before, with one exception. It was the day Gautier offered a spell that set his flesh to flames and a moment of utter agony that he would never forget.

Confused by the heat, he looked up at the dark sky searching for the sun. He knew it had set long before he had jumped from the ship, for he had clearly seen the moon and the stars in the night's sky. Something or someone was controlling the heat. Desperate for shelter, he looked left and then right but found nothing but trees as far as he could see. Deciding the shade of the trees was better than nothing, he trudged through the coarse sand hoping to ease his discomfort.

Sitting in the darkness, he leaned back against the rough bulging roots of a tree. He willed the heat to leave his senses, but there was no escaping it. He had heard tales of places that were covered in sand and consumed by heat. If it offered the same sensations or worse, he knew it would not be a place that he would be willing to explore.

Closing his eyes, he tried to put his mind at ease. After all, the spell had been broken, and he had escaped. He was no longer a prisoner of Black Thistle Castle or Alltree Island. He was finally free. Feeling his body relax, he drifted off to sleep.

It was a rhythmic sound that caught his attention and drew him from his deep slumber. He knew the sound of pounding hooves and knew they were heading in his direction. Jumping up, he looked for a place to hide as he reached for where his dagger used to be. The absence of it made him pause, and the thought of it drew a tightness around his heart causing him to stumble. With his hand pressed against the rough bark of a tree, he suddenly remembered his gift of haze. He calmed his senses and reached for the gift that would make him invisible, but nothing happened. Stunned at his loss, he looked down at his trembling hands.

Three guards straddling black stallions suddenly broke through the trees. In one swift movement, they all dismounted and stood before Jario. Dressed in crimson with silver breastplates bearing black swans, the men stood an ax handle taller than Jario. He had never seen men of such stature and wondered if they were men or merely beasts in disguise. They wore black helmets allowing only their eyes and mouth to be exposed, small leather wings covered their ears, and four sharp appendages stood making what appeared to be a crown above their foreheads. Jario surmised their function was meant only to instill fear in their victim, and they had done their job. He was sure he had fallen prey to something evil.

"You are ordered by Mistress Violeta to stand before her," a guard declared, as he stepped forward.

"I have done nothing. Had I not come ashore, I would have drowned in the sea," Jario replied, hoping for some sense of understanding. "I was but a passenger on the *Withering Rose*. I am sure you know this island was not its destination."

"Save your breath, for I have no power to release you. It will be for the mistress to decide your future. Until then, you are in my charge and a prisoner of the Firelight Army."

Jario's arms were quickly pulled behind his back and shackles put around his wrists. Before he could object, he was easily thrown upon the back of a stallion behind one of the silent guards. Regretting his decision to leave the *Withering Rose*, Jario felt the heavy weight of dread and helplessness to save himself.

* * *

The chamber that held Mistress Violeta's throne and the seats of her four counselors was dark. After the sun had given way to the rising of the moon, she had long since made her way up the stone steps to her bedchamber to be alone. The recent death of Aodh (pronounced A-odd), her loving companion, had caused the flame in her heart to quiet. Without it, her body felt ice-cold.

The fire in her hearth roared to life, and she stepped closer in hopes of feeling its warmth. Finding little comfort in its vibrant flames, she turned and made her way toward the doors to her balcony. Reaching for the ornate metal handles, she drew the doors open and stepped out into the night air. Lifting her chin, she could feel a warm breeze against her face, and she pretended it was the gentle caress of Aodh's fingertips. A tear slipped from the corner of her eye as she closed her eyes and remembered the amber flecks within his green eyes.

The sound of a ship's bell drew her from her thoughts, and she took in the sight of the glowing lanterns that swayed on what she knew was the *Withering Rose*. She had been standing on the sand one evening as it passed and admired the carved figurehead of a man's bare shoulder with an outstretched arm holding a dagger that pierced a rose. She often wondered if a lady had thrown the rose to her lover, or he was purely offering her his broken heart.

Suddenly, the trees along the shore flared their warning. Violeta knew that someone had stepped upon the island's warm sand. Furious with this intrusion, she ran from her balcony toward her chamber door. Flinging it open, she hurried down the stone steps scarcely feeling them beneath her soft leather slippers.

"Angus, we have intruders," she cried.

He met her at the bottom of the stone steps and grasped her arm to steady her. Looking into her amber eyes, he saw her fear.

"Mistress, we saw the flare. The guards are on their way," he softly replied, trying to calm her.

"What if he is another man sent by the evil wizard, Jessop? The last man he sent was cunning. He was able to hide who he was from me, and my sweet Aodh paid the price for my failure to recognize the danger."

"You have nothing to fear. The spell upon the trees has undoubtedly stolen any powers that the intruder possesses. The guards will bring him here to stand before you. If need be, the Ravens will do your bidding. He will be completely honest, or he will die."

Violeta looked up at Angus and nodded.

"Let's get you to your throne," he urged her forward. "They will be here soon."

* * *

Angus stood next to Violeta as she sat gripping the arms of her throne. Her back straightened as the guards brought in the intruder. With his wrists secured behind his back, they gripped his upper arms and forced him to his knees before her.

Without raising his head, he could see the crimson hem of her gown and the toes of her pointed slippers. She appeared to be a tiny thing. The silence was killing him, but he thought it best to wait for permission to speak.

"Who are you, and why are you here?" Violeta sternly asked.

Jario raised his head to look at the woman that spoke to him. Her beauty took his breath away. Her hair, the color of raven wings, hung in soft curls against her fair skin, and her lips were painted to match her gown. Her amber eyes seemed to glow; however, it was the glowing violet light where her heart should be that caught his eye.

"I asked you a question?" she snapped, impatiently waiting for an answer.

Before he could answer, he felt a guard's hand smack the back of his head pushing him forward. He groaned as he landed hard on his shoulder before immediately being jerked back up to his knees.

"My Lady, my name is Jario. I am from Alltree Island."

Violeta knew of Alltree Island and the peace that they desired. She had heard the rumors from those that came ashore.

"What brings you to the Isle of Flames?"

"I know you will find this odd, but the light in the tower drew me here. I jumped from the *Withering Rose* and swam to your shore. I have not been well, since."

"The sickness you speak of tells me that you have given up your powers. You should know that I have ways of finding out what they are, but it would be much easier on you if you would tell me of them."

Jario knew that this would be his undoing and closed his eyes regretting stepping foot on the island.

"I'm waiting," she snapped.

"I am a vampire that has learned to survive on animal blood. It was forbidden within the walls of the Evergreen Castle to drink human blood. It was Lady Lara's one rule, and it was never to be broken."

Jario watched her face, but her expression never changed. Seeing her nod, he knew she wanted him to continue.

"My gifts consist of the ability to become invisible by using haze, turning objects or people to stone, compulsion, and changing my appearance. I lost my gift of smoke to a vampire called Balgair."

Jario saw her rake her teeth across her bottom lip and then look up at the man that stood beside her. Without speaking, he could tell that something passed between them. Slowly she stood and clasped her hands in front of her.

"Jario, you are to be taken to the dungeon. I believe there is more to your story, and I intend to find out who has sent you."

The guards gripped his arms and stood him on his feet.

"My Lady, I mean you no harm," he blurted, as the guards

dragged him away. "Take me to the sand. I will jump back into the sea and never bother you again."

His cries for mercy echoed through the hallways until silence offered Violeta great relief. She looked at Angus and smiled.

"He was drawn by the light, Angus," she sighed. "He must be the one that is destined to retrieve the *Singing Sword*. If he is, I will have my freedom at last."

* * *

Thirteen moons have passed since Jario left Alltree Island and found himself a prisoner in the Firelight Castle's dungeon. Sitting in the darkness, he has set his mind to wondering if Mistress Violeta would ever show him mercy. To leave the Isle of Flames is his only desire, and for that privilege, he would do anything she asked of him. It is the only thing he has left to offer for his freedom. Until that desire is granted, he sits alone with nothing to think about except his past. It was the past he had hoped to forget since it was full of nothing but failures.

Chapter 2

The Arrival

Baxter followed closely behind Laralynn riding astride Starlight as they emerged from the cool shadows of the Evergreen Forest. The sun was high in the sky, and it caused Laralynn to shield her eyes allowing her to take in the vivid colors of the meadow.

"I love this meadow when it is full of wildflowers and tall swaying grass," she sighed. "The scent is glorious." In what seemed like a response, her mare raised and lowered her head in a nodding motion. "I believe she agrees with me; however, I think she fancies the taste of its sweet grass more than its scent."

Baxter smiled knowing the only scent he ever noticed was that of Laralynn's. To him, the scent of fresh apples was intoxicating.

"Are you up for some fun?" laughed Laralynn. "Let's race to Black Thistle?"

"What's my prize if I win?" he countered.

"What makes you think you'll win?"

"If I do, what's my prize?"

"Hmm, a walk in the moonlight with me, and a kiss is my offering."

"I'll take that wager and that prize."

"What if I win? What prize do you offer?"

"A walk in the moonlight with me, and a kiss would be my offering as well."

"Just one kiss?"

"I could be persuaded to sweeten the pot with more than one."

"Then let's ride on my count. I'm aiming to win that prize."

Laralynn calmly stated one and then two. Giving Baxter a wicked smile, she nudged Starlight with the heels of her boots, and they sped forward. Looking over her shoulder, she shouted three. She could hear him cursing as he chased after her.

It wasn't long before Black Thistle Castle was in sight. With their horses even, they skirted the thistles as they headed for the drawbridge. Looking down at the moat, Baxter slowed as he remembered a time, not so long ago, when it had held thick black mud and slithered with something that appeared to be alive. Since that time, the darkness had been driven away and no longer existed. It now contained nothing but water and rocks covered in moss.

"I win!" shouted Laralynn as she passed through Black Thistle's gate and dismounted her mare while watching Baxter ride toward her.

He dismounted and stroked the neck of his stallion. "Looks like I owe you a prize."

They both turned when they heard the heavy wooden doors open, and Gustavo quickly making his way down the steps to greet them.

"Lady Laralynn, I am glad that you have come," he said, with worry filling his eyes. "Alicia's time is near, and she has labored long with no reward. Might you visit her?"

"Of course, take me to her bedchamber," she replied, as she followed Gustavo up the steps. "Baxter, go find Killian and ease his mind."

* * *

Killian paced the dimly lit hallway outside their bedchamber. He had listened to Alicia struggle through the pain of childbirth for hours. If it hadn't been for Baxter and Gustavo, Killian would have broken down the door at her first whimper. He was thrilled the day she came to him to announce that she was with child, and their wolves had celebrated with a moonlit run. At the time, the thought of having a child sounded exciting and easy. Now, he knew better. He was utterly terrified.

The sound of a babe's cry caused Killian to reach for the handle of the door.

"I have to see Alicia and my child," pleaded Killian.

"Wait," cautioned Gustavo. "There is much that must be done before you may enter. Your lady will want the look of labor washed from her face before she lays the babe in your arms."

Nodding, he understood and stepped back. It seemed as if only a moment had passed, and he heard another babe's cry. Killian turned toward Baxter with his mouth agape.

"Well done, Killian. Well done," Baxter said, as he slapped him on the shoulder. "You are a potent one to be sure."

"This is a grand reward that she has given you, Killian," Gustavo said, as he offered his hand in congratulations.

"Two . . . Two babes? I never expected two babes."

"Be joyful Killian, your blessings have been multiplied," Baxter offered, when he saw the look of worry on his face.

"'Tis true, it is a blessing. I just didn't expect so many in one day."

Gustavo and Baxter laughed as they embraced their friend.

Hearing the door open, the men turned to see Laralynn standing in the doorway. Killian nervously stepped forward.

"Killian, are you ready to meet your babes?" she asked.

Laralynn stepped back allowing him to enter. He slowly moved toward the bed and saw that Alicia sat propped against large feather pillows holding a babe in each arm. He noticed the hair around her face was still damp, and her braid hung over one shoulder with a white ribbon woven through it.

"Are you well, my love?" he asked, as he sat on the edge of the bed and stroked her cheek with the back of his hand.

"To my surprise, I find that I am much better than I expected. I am thankful for Lady Laralynn's arrival, and her healing touch."

"And the babes?"

"The babes are perfect. They have the proper amount of fingers and toes. Their eyes are blue like the midday sky, and their cries are strong. We have been blessed with a son and a daughter."

"You have outdone yourself. I could not have asked for more."

"Would you like to hold your son?"

Before he could respond, Alicia's mother picked up the babe and placed him in his arms.

"He is so tiny, and he is light as a feather. What shall we name him?"

"I have chosen Faolan (pronounced Fway-lawn). It means wolf gift. Does it please you?"

"It is a good name and a strong name. What name have you given our daughter?"

"I have chosen Eirlys (pronounced Air-lees). It means snowdrop."

"Snowdrop? I'm not sure I understand why you have chosen such an unusual name?"

Alicia pulled the blanket away from their daughter's head to reveal a small tuft of white hair that had been tied with a piece of white lace.

"I see; her hair is the color of snow."

As they all laughed at his surprise, Lord Gautier and Lady Kayleigh quietly entered the chamber.

"May we intrude?" asked Gautier.

Killian stood and turned, still holding his son.

"Lord Gautier, Lady Kayleigh, of course, you may. Come and see. Alicia has given me a sturdy son and a beautiful daughter."

He gently lowered his son into Lady Kayleigh's arms and watched her lovingly kiss his forehead.

"What are their names?" asked Kayleigh.

"We have named our son Faolan and our daughter Eirlys."

"Faolan, you are very handsome," whispered Kayleigh.

"I see Eirlys has been given the gift of white hair. It is said that babes born with white hair are filled with wisdom," explained Gautier. "We will have much to learn from her, and if Faolan is like his father, he will be a great guardian someday as well."

Killian was touched by their words and beamed with pride.

Kayleigh handed Faolan back to Killian and looked at Alicia as she asked, "Are you well?"

"Well enough," she replied. "To do this twice in one day was quite a surprise."

"When you are strong again, I would like to celebrate the birth of your babes. It has been some time since we have had a reason to celebrate. I believe your wedding was the last time if I am not mistaken. How does a masquerade ball sound to you?" asked Gautier.

"Lord Gautier, it sounds wonderful," Alicia replied.

"Then it is settled. When you are strong enough, we will fill the Great Hall with music, laughter, and fanciful masks. It will be great fun."

"Gautier, we should go now and let Alicia rest," whispered Kayleigh.

"Of course, my dear. What was I thinking? We wish you both congratulations on the birth of your son and daughter. May they bring you much joy," Gautier said, as he clasped Kayleigh's hand.

As they turned to leave, Laralynn, Baxter, and Gustavo followed close behind.

Alicia's mother leaned down and kissed her daughter's forehead. "You have done well, my daughter. I will leave you two alone to get to know your children." After brushing the hair from Killian's eyes, she smiled and walked toward the door.

As Killian sat down on the edge of the bed, he heard the bedchamber door close.

"I love you, Alicia. You have given me the most remarkable gifts," he said, as tears ran from his eyes.

Chapter 3

The Task

Jario sat with his arms wrapped tightly around his legs on a mattress stuffed with sour straw feeling like a caged animal. Knowing it was time for the guard to bring him his meal, he could feel his throat screaming for blood. His days had constantly been spent listening for the sound of the guard's boots that would announce his arrival and that of the luscious liquid that would offer him momentary relief. Jario realized today would be like many others, and he rested his head against his knees trying to ignore the pain of hunger.

Deep within the hallways of the dungeon, a faint sound of something familiar caught his attention. He could sense the guard's possible arrival, and it made his fangs descend and pierce his bottom lip. It wasn't until he heard the sound of metal keys striking against each other that his hope turned to yearning. He sat quietly as the rusty hinges groaned, and the heavy dungeon door scraped against the stone floor as it opened. Light from a burning torch brightened Jario's dimly lit cell. He lifted his head to see the outline of a huge man standing before him.

"You have been ordered to stand before Mistress Violeta," barked the guard. "Stand and turn your back to the cell door. I have brought shackles for your wrists."

Without hesitation, Jario jumped from his bed and stood with his hands behind his back. This was the first opportunity he had been given since his imprisonment to face Mistress Violeta, and he would not do anything careless to ruin it. His cell door opened, and he felt the weight of the iron cuffs clasped about his wrists and the thick chain drawn around his waist. A large hand grasped his upper arm firmly and turned him toward the open cell.

He tried to remember the path from his cell, but the twists and turns of the hallways left his mind muddled. Giving up on any chance of escape, he tried to focus on what he might say to his new mistress; however, the light ahead of him caused him to halt.

"The sunlight shines through the tall narrow windows. It spills upon the floor and the wall. There are no shadows. I cannot take this path," Jario blurted, as he tried to yank himself free of the guard's hold.

"It is only a few windows," the guard grumbled.

"I beg you not to take me this way."

The guard looked at the sunlight filling the hallway and back at Jario. He tightened his grip on Jario's arm and pulled him forward.

"You don't understand. The sunlight will give me my final death."

"Cover him," bellowed a voice from the far end of the hallway.

The men turned to see Angus walking toward them.

"I said cover him. Do it quickly. Mistress Violeta is waiting."

The guard released Jario's arm and pulled his crimson tabard over his head. With Angus' supervision, he wrapped its length about Jario's body and covered his head. Sure that he would be protected, the guard threw him over his shoulder and followed Angus briskly through the hallway past the light filled windows.

Jario could feel the heat across his back and the back of his legs, but it was nothing compared to what he had experienced in the past. The protection of the tabard had been a kind gesture offered to him, and he would not forget it.

When the guard's tabard was removed, Jario found himself standing before two wooden doors. Each elaborately carved door bore a black swan. One held the stem of a rose yet to bloom and the other a dagger studded with rubies. As he gazed at the swans, he was sure he had seen the ruffle of their feathers. He took a step back fearing his mind had left him.

"Your wrists," ordered the guard.

Jario did not move and stared again at the swans.

"Your wrists, I need your wrists," demanded the guard.

Mindlessly, he raised his hands and felt the cuffs released from his wrists, and the chain removed from his waist.

"You will walk beside me and kneel on my command. When the mistress enters the chamber, you will bow your head. Speak only when you are asked to speak. Be mindful that I am quick with a dagger and won't hesitate to use it," demanded Angus.

"I understand," replied Jario.

The doors swung open, and Jario took in the dark chamber lit only by candles. Noticing the draperies had been drawn to shield the sunlight, he sighed with relief. Jario walked beside Angus until he was commanded to stop and kneel. Doing as he was commanded, he waited for Mistress Violeta to take her place on her throne. It wasn't long before he heard a door open and the rustle of several layers of fabric. He quickly bowed his head and waited. He could hear her sit and straighten her gown. Daring to raise his eyes, he caught a glimpse of her silver slippers from beneath the hem of her skirt.

"It is time for me to make my demands known," she said, as she tapped her nails against the arms of her throne. "I am sure that you are eager to leave this island, and to be sure, I am eager for your release. You may raise your head so that I might see your eyes. I need to be sure that you understand everything I demand of you."

Jario raised his head and took in the beauty of the woman that sat before him. She was dressed in a red gown that shimmered in the candlelight. Her black hair glistened like a raven's wing, and it had been woven with silver ribbons and tiny red rosebuds. The amber eyes that he remembered from the first time they met were now violet and matched the violet light that pulsed over her heart.

"Have you studied me enough?" Violeta tilted her head with curiosity. "Do you find me pleasing, little vampire?"

Jario quickly lowered his eyes. "My Lady, forgive me. I have seen nothing but darkness for a very long time. It pleased me to look upon your beauty."

"You have sweet words, but will they still be sweet when I tell you what I need from you?"

Jario raised his chin and straightened his shoulders. "You need only ask, and I will obey your command."

Her laughter sent chills slithering up his spine, and he could feel the hairs on his arms stand on end as he watched her stand.

"I have decided to let you leave this island, and your gifts will be returned to you. In return for my kindness, I will require something from you."

"My Lady, anything," gasped Jario. "You need only name it."

"You are to bring me the *Singing Sword.*"

Jario furrowed his brow and searched his mind. "I know nothing of the *Singing Sword.*"

"It has been called many things throughout hundreds of years. Some have called it the *Voice of Silver* and the *Lyrics of Strength.* You may know it as *Fuaim na Cumhacta* or *Sound of Power.* It is a simple sword that might hang from a lad's hip. Most would pay it no mind and pass it by."

Jario searched his mind for the words she had spoken. It was familiar, but he couldn't recall where he had heard the words. As he whispered the words, it all came back to him. The sword she desired was hanging on the wall in the hidden chamber of Black Thistle Castle, and it would surely mean his final death if he returned to retrieve it.

"I see that you know of what I speak."

"I have touched the sword and heard its strange humming sound. I have read the engraving, but to try and retrieve this sword would mean I would forfeit my life. The castle belongs to a warlock, and a witch has offered to protect all within it."

"I find we have a predicament before us. You fear that the task is too dangerous, and you will receive your final death if you go to this castle to retrieve the sword. If you don't retrieve it, I will be forced to give you your final death in my dungeon for your refusal. It is your choice. Which do you prefer?"

"My Lady, I will go to the Black Thistle Castle and retrieve the sword."

"Excellent, your decision pleases me. You are a wise little vampire."

Happy with his response, Violeta returned to her throne.

"Jario, please stand."

As he did, a bright light blinded him for a moment. His body suddenly felt refreshed as if he had stood under a waterfall. Lifting his arms, he discovered his once ragged clothing had been replaced with a fine linen tunic, soft leather breeches, and knee-high black boots. A dagger was sheathed at his hip, a pouch heavy with coin hung from a leather belt, and a medallion bearing a black swan hung around his neck.

"My Lady, I thank you for these fine gifts. You have been very generous."

"Once you have completed the task, you will receive a great reward." She could see Jario's eyes light up. She knew the look of greed and had seen it in many a man's eyes. "On your return, you will be given what you have desired for so long. You will be gifted a magnificent castle, servants, great wealth, and all the power you desire. This is my promise to you."

The sound of boots echoed through the hall, and Jario turned to see the guards coming toward him.

"My guards will escort you to the sea, and a boat awaits to take you to the *Withering Rose* that is anchored not far from this island." She could see him hiding a sly grin and knew what he was thinking. "Do not attempt to betray me, for I will know of it. You see, the medallion you wear around your neck will allow my guards to find you. You will not be allowed to remove it."

As Jario ran his fingers over the face of the medallion, it slowly disappeared from view.

"It is safely hidden within your chest. If you try to remove it, it will pierce your heart, and you will die. Now, go find the sword and bring it back to me."

Struggling to make sense of everything he had heard, Jario turned to leave but stopped when he heard her start to speak.

"Oh, I forgot something vital to your survival. You must complete this task within nine full moons. If you fail, the medallion you wear will give you your final death."

The guards escorted Jario from the hall toward what he assumed would be the door that would open to the courtyard. Fearing these guards had not planned for the sunlight, he halted and refused to move forward.

"We have our orders. You are to be taken to the boat," a guard said, as he reached for Jario's arm.

"I can't go into the sunlight. It will mean my death. If I am dead, I surely cannot complete the task that lies ahead of me."

"You have nothing to fear. The medallion my mistress has given you will protect you. Why would she forfeit her chance to claim the *Singing Sword* with your death? You have not even attempted to complete your task."

Jario listened to the guard's explanation and was certain the medallion held some special powers. If nothing else, he was assured it would claim his life if he failed. Trusting the guards, he walked through the open doors and into the bright sunlight. Feeling only the warmth of the sun's rays upon his face, he amused himself by holding out his arms and facing the sun.

"I shall enjoy this most of all," he laughed, as he accepted the reins to a black stallion draped in crimson silks.

"Your ship is waiting. We have no time to waste," stated the guard.

Eager to discover what else the medallion provided, Jario mounted his stallion and raced behind the guards toward the sea. Trees lined the twisted path creating a canopy of branches filled with amber, red, and orange leaves as far as he could see.

With the color of the trees and the heat of this island, it was now obvious to him why the island bore the name Isle of Flames.

As they reached the sea, he could see the *Withering Rose* anchored a short distance from the shore. A small boat rested in the coarse sand waiting to take him from the island. He dismounted and handed the reins of his stallion to a guard's outstretched hand. Looking back at the tops of the trees, he saw the tower of the Firelight Castle and a flash of light from its window.

"Did you see that flash of light?" asked Jario. "I saw that same light from the deck of the ship. It is what drew me to this island."

"It is merely the mistress in the tower," the guard responded. "Now, off with you."

Jario climbed into the boat with a guard just as it slipped into the water. An intoxicating breeze swirled around his head. Looking back at the tower, he saw her standing on a small balcony. As the breeze warmed, he could hear her whisper, "Do not fail me. I will not tolerate failure."

Not knowing if she could hear him, he whispered his reply, "When I return, I will lay the *Singing Sword* at your feet and proudly accept my reward."

As the small boat neared the *Withering Rose*, Jario bowed his head and covered his face with his hands. He searched for the power that would allow him to change his appearance. A subtle tingling sensation crept across his torso, up his neck, and over his face to the top of his head. An image of a man with olive complexion, shoulder length dark hair tied at the nape of his neck, and warm brown eyes appeared in his mind. Satisfied that he would not be recognized, he let the image consume his body and lifted his hands from his face.

"The change is a good one," the guard laughed, as he steered the boat alongside the ship. "The ladies will be sure to like it."

Gripping the rope ladder, Jario began the climb that would see him aboard the ship that would carry him back to Alltree

Island and the *Singing Sword.*

Chapter 4

The Warning

Laralynn moaned as she felt the impact of her body being slammed to the floor. Raising up on her elbows, she looked at Elda and shook her head.

"Will I ever be able to take you down?" groaned Laralynn.

"Not if I have anything to say about it," Elda replied, as she offered Laralynn her hand. "If you did, everyone would think I let you. They all know that I have rarely lost a fight."

Accepting her hand, Laralynn rested the sole of her boot against the toe of Elda's boot for leverage to stand. Instead, she jerked Elda forward flipping her over her shoulder to the floor.

"I finally did it!" squealed Laralynn. Jumping up she bowed to her cheering audience, but her glee was cut short. She noticed the smirk on Elda's face and knew she was in for some future trouble. "Elda, I'm sorry, but I had to try it. I didn't think I'd be able to do it, but I had to try."

Elda stood and rubbed the back of her head. "I didn't think you could catch me off-guard, but you did. Remember that trick. It may come in handy."

"It isn't often you will find Elda on her back," laughed Tate.

"Uncle, you were watching?"

"I just entered the Command Center in time to see you toss

Elda onto her back. It was a first for me and quite the surprise. Enjoy your success, for I doubt she will ever allow it to happen again."

Feeling a shiver of annoyance that stiffened her shoulders, Elda started to walk away.

"Wait, Elda, I have come to bring you and Laralynn to the Council Chamber. Lady Lara has asked for both of you to listen to the news she has received."

As Laralynn entered the chamber, she saw Meadow to the left of her mother. Her hands were clasped and rested on the table. A smile greeted her, but the look of worry rested upon her face. Taking a seat, she glanced at her mother and saw her take her father's hand. With a sudden sense of dread, her hands began to tremble, and she quickly lowered them to her lap.

"Meadow has come to us with some disturbing news. It appears that Jario is on his way to Alltree Island," announced Thomas.

"I thought we were rid of that traitorous vampire," blurted Oliver.

"After he managed to escape, I was sure he wouldn't return. There is nothing left for him here. If he is indeed on his way back to Alltree, it may not be of his choosing," Lara suggested. "Meadow, please tell them what you have already told me."

Meadow unclasped her hands and pointed to the corner of the chamber. A large thick book removed itself from an ornate wooden pedestal and floated through the air above Oliver's head to the surface of the long table. Everyone watched as the soft leather cover of the book rippled and then opened. Meadow tapped her finger twice on the table, and the pages began to turn. One by one, the pages turned faster and faster. When they came to a sudden stop, Meadow made a snapping sound with her tongue and shook her head. A single page began to flutter and slowly turned itself over.

Satisfied, Meadow began to speak. "It is common knowledge that my dreams are filled with visions, and they are not always pleasant. They are very much like your dreams, but my dreams are of things to come. I have seen Jario in my dreams."

"Would it be too much trouble to give the traitor his final death in one of your dreams?" laughed Oliver.

"Quiet!" barked Thomas.

"I am sorry My Lord," replied Oliver.

"Meadow, please continue," urged Lara.

"He has left the Isle of Flames and travels on the *Withering Rose*. He stands in the sunlight and wears a talisman of some kind that affords him this power. But, it also carries the threat of his demise. I do not know his quest, but I can assume he would not hesitate to cause someone harm to complete it."

"Why have you laid this book before us?" asked Laralynn.

"Upon these pages are written what is known of a woman named Violeta. She has been the Mistress of Firelight Castle for hundreds of years and lives on the Isle of Flames. Like our Gavenia, she is a shifter; however, her spirit is that of a black swan. Her father forbade her to wed a young man named Ewan, who was also a black swan shifter. She loved him beyond all others and promised her heart would always belong to him. Her father was a greedy man and had grander prospects for his daughter that would offer him great wealth. To keep her from running away with Ewan, he purchased a binding spell from the Wizard Jessop. Since that time, she has been bound to the island and seeking the one thing that will allow her to leave, a *Singing Sword*."

"What of her father?" asked Baxter. "Has his heart not softened with time?"

"He was mysteriously poisoned after a wealthy suitor discovered her father was auctioning Violeta to the highest bidder. The death of her father has left her trapped on the island unless someone can find the sword or a loophole to break the curse."

"I am sure you have all made the connection, just as I have. Violeta has sent Jario to find the *Singing Sword*, and he believes it is on this island," proposed Thomas.

"Does anyone know of this sword?" asked Baxter.

Everyone at the table shook their heads.

"Then, we need to find it before he does," continued Baxter. "I am willing to bet there is some great reward offered to him if he finds it. He does nothing unless it is to his benefit."

"If we find it first, we can set a trap to capture him and return the sword to Violeta," reasoned Laralynn. "We have to help her."

"Preston, make sure that Echo Bluff and the surrounding villages are safe. Send word to Lord Gautier that Jario is heading to the island. Jario may have a quest, but revenge may also be on his mind. We will need men posted at the harbors. If we can catch him as he steps off the *Withering Rose*, we will be better for it," ordered Thomas.

"As you wish, My Lord," replied Preston.

"Jario is a danger to all of us. His gift of stone left Killian to suffer for some time, and as Laralynn discovered, he can change his appearance," Lara added.

"He won't be easy to capture, but Laralynn is right," agreed Thomas. "If we find the sword first, we can use it to our advantage. Let's get our plans in order and prepare for the trouble Jario is sure to offer us."

Everyone responded by pounding their fists on the table before they stood and made their way to the doorway.

"There is one good thing in all of this," Elda smiled, as she backed her chair away from the table and moved to let Preston and Baxter pass.

"What is that?" asked Laralynn.

"He won't get any help from Velsa."

Laralynn frowned. She knew Elda was right, but it only reminded her of poor lonely Aslev and that she hadn't visited her in a long time.

"Laralynn," sighed her mother. "Come here, child."

She stood before her mother and felt her kiss her forehead before she whispered in her ear, "Elda did not mean to hurt your feelings. Not everyone thinks of Aslev as you do."

"I know mother, but it still hurts. She was very kind to me, and I know that she loved me."

"Why don't you and Baxter ride to Primrose Pond and visit Aslev, Astra, and your friends. Tell them of our anticipated visitor. It will help Preston get the word out about Jario to the villages beyond Whistler's River."

"Mother, you always know the right thing to say to make me feel better."

"Be ever careful in your travels. Jario could be anywhere, and he could be wearing a face that you may not recognize."

"I will not let him fool me, mother. I am no longer the naive and foolish child he lied to at the pond near our cottage. You see; I have the upper hand. I know his gifts, and he knows not one of mine. He will be very surprised, don't you think?"

"Do not take his gifts lightly, my child. We all saw what happened to Killian. One touch from him could turn you to stone."

"I promise to be careful."

* * *

Aslev knelt among the flowers and herbs in her garden. She seemed to have an unusual fondness for the sprigs of green that grew prolifically among the flowers. She had taken to hanging bundles of her favorite herbs, rosemary and thyme, at her window. To her delight, the sun's rays coming through her window warmed the herbs, and their scent permeated her cottage. It was Astra that had shown her how to twist the herbs into wreaths that she traded for goods at the market. It was a satisfying chore that she found chased away some of the pain that muddled her mind.

Off in the distance, the dull thudding sound of what she thought were horse's hooves against the dirt road caused her to stand. She had very few visitors, but only a few that came on horseback. She dropped her cuttings into her basket and wiped her dirty hands on her apron as she hurried to the gate to greet her visitors.

"Aslev, how are you this fine day?" asked Laralynn. She dismounted Starlight and tied her reins to the wooden post of the fence.

"I am much happier now that I see your smiling faces," Aslev replied, as she wrapped her arms around Laralynn and kissed her forehead. "Come inside, you both must be thirsty after your ride."

Baxter and Laralynn followed Aslev into her cottage, and each dipped the large wooden spoon in the pail of water for a drink before they handed the spoon back to Aslev.

"Do I smell sweet cakes?" asked Laralynn.

"You do, indeed. I made the little cakes fresh this morning. It will only take me a moment to heat the water for tea. Sit and tell me all you have learned since your last visit."

"Keep it simple," Baxter spoke into Laralynn's mind. "Do not say a word about Jario."

"There is some exciting news. Killian and Alicia have had twin babes. I have seen them, and they are the tiniest things."

"There are many tales of twins. Their parents should be mindful," warned Aslev.

"Mindful of what?" asked Laralynn.

"It is said that one will be evil and one good."

"That could be said of any siblings," suggested Baxter. "Not everyone sees the world the same way."

"I find your logic true. I only repeat what has been passed down through time. It comes from those that have known tales of woe," replied Aslev.

"I am sure Faolan and Eirlys will both be good. How can they help being good? Killian and Alicia are both good souls," declared Laralynn.

"Let's not speak of trouble. We have a cake to eat," laughed Aslev as she placed the pot of tea and the tray of warm, sweet cakes on the table. "Baxter, will you pour the tea? I find my hands are too unsteady today."

As Baxter reached for the pot, a rap on the door caused his hand to go to the dagger at his hip.

"Who stands at my door?" shouted Aslev.

"Aslev, it is Astra," she called out.

"Put your hand at ease, young man. You worry too much," fussed Aslev. "There is no danger here. It is only Astra."

Baxter watched as Aslev welcomed Astra with a warm embrace. It still seemed odd to see Aslev's love for her sister. He wouldn't blame Astra if she held some resentment for being banished to the mountain. He knew he wouldn't have been so forgiving of a spell that cursed him to a mountain. But, Astra was different; she could forgive anyone. She was a kind and loving soul. She knew that Aslev's magic and memories disappeared that day in front of her cottage, and as a result, it was a chance to start over.

Astra happily joined them for tea and sweet cakes. Laralynn passed along the news of the twins and the masquerade ball Lord Gautier had announced to celebrate their birth. Astra spoke of her fondness for Oliver with the promise that Baxter would not speak a word of it to Oliver. All in all, it was an afternoon of friendly conversation that brought a smile to everyone's faces.

As they were ready to leave, Baxter pulled Astra aside to warn her of Jario's return to Alltree and to ask her to keep an eye out for any strangers that might visit Aslev. He felt certain that Jario would try and find his old friend Velsa for help and was fearful of what things would be triggered in her mind if he did.

Chapter 5

A New Identity

It was the pointed roof of the Old Stone Tower standing far above the treetops that told him they would soon be entering Woods Bay. Just the sight of it offered him much-needed relief. Not only would he finally be leaving the dark, cramped quarters of the *Withering Rose*, but he would be put ashore far from the Evergreen Castle and their annoying army.

As he leaned against the ship's railings, he thought back to the day he had awakened on the stone floor of Black Thistle Castle. Something strange had happened that day. A loud blast had shaken the earth beneath the castle and caused the shield that held him cursed inside his dagger to fall to the floor. Suddenly free from the curse, granted only by some loophole, he watched as flapping banners, burning torches, and crumbling stained glass fell to the floor of the Great Hall. While making his escape, he had seen the stones that had fallen from the walls surrounding the castle and the black thistles that lay withered upon the ground. It was unlike anything he had ever seen, and he hoped to see nothing like it again. He needed to know what had caused it, and there was no one better to explain this mystery to him than the witch, Velsa.

Pacing back and forth at the bow of the ship, Jario set his mind to work. He needed a plan and a new identity that would allow him entry into Black Thistle Castle. The skills of a craftsman would easily let him through the gate, but he would then be relegated to the people's quarters until someone needed something from him. To be honest, he was no craftsman, and others would quickly discover him as a fraud. He needed an identity that held a station high enough to make his entry into the castle unquestionable. A lord or lord's champion would allow him the entry he needed, but he would hail from where? It had to be far enough away that no one would know he was lying. He had to think quickly; the ship would be docking soon.

Slapping his hand against the railings, he suddenly had an idea. He could be a Trade Emissary. It would grant him a meeting with a member of the council within the castle. From there, he could pull his haze and make his way to the hidden chamber. Once he retrieved the sword, he would make his way to the harbor and sail away undetected. A few days were all he needed, and he could easily claim his reward. But, he would need a name. It would need to be something regal sounding and something befitting a Trade Emissary.

"Quinsley sounds regal but not regal enough," he mumbled under his breath. He quickly looked about to see if anyone had heard him. He laughed as he thought about the name. "It sounds like a measly servant's name. What about Sir Weston Quinsley? That is much better. Maybe a Duke would be a more fitting title. The Duke of what? The Duke of Remonnet has a certain flare to it. But, from where? It needs to be something I won't forget." As he thought about the places and things he had seen, he suddenly remembered the white hawk. "If only I could see you again, my sweet white hawk." He closed his eyes and pictured her perched upon the post of his bed looking down at him. "In your honor, I will claim Hawk Perch Island as my home."

Before he knew it, the *Withering Rose* had docked, and the smack of the gangplank startled him as it echoed in the harbor. "I find this Duke is quite eager to discover what he has missed since he has been away," laughed Jario. "I think I might play awhile before I steal that precious sword. After all, I have plenty of time, and I yearn for the pleasures that I have missed while held prisoner."

Not wanting to waste a moment of it, Jario made his way to the dock. As he waited for the small trunk that the guards sent with him, he secured a man that sat upon an empty wagon to carry him to the local tavern. Once there, he would be sure to secure a room and purchase a horse from the stable. Climbing onto the wooden bench, he leaned back crossing his arms over his chest. Closing his eyes, he raised his face toward the sun to absorb its warmth and sighed.

The ride to the village had been short and easy enough. Jumping from the wagon, he took in the sounds and smells coming from the weathered tavern. The driver retrieved his trunk and set it beside him.

"Will you be need'n me to carry yer trunk, sir?" asked the driver. "It would not be fit'n fur a fine man such as you to be left wit' such a chore."

Jario frowned. He knew the man wanted a coin or two more for his effort, and it annoyed him to the bone. Ready to curse at the man, he suddenly remembered his new station. He gave the man a nod and headed for the door.

Bertha was the first to notice the handsome newcomer coming through the door. She quickly untied her soiled apron and tossed it on the corner of the bar. Taking a moment to adjust her ample bosom and tuck the stray hairs behind her ears, she made her way to greet him.

"Good day fine sir," she said, as sweetly as she could. "What can I do fur you today?"

Jario smiled at the woman and gave her a polite bow to impress her. "I'll be needing a room for a few days, maybe more. It will depend on how quickly I can complete my business venture here on the island."

"And your business venture would be?" she asked, with trepidation in her voice. "If you be a bounty-hunter, I want no trouble. These are fair and decent men that sit about my tavern.

I board no criminals here, good sir."

"I am no bounty-hunter, Madame." Jario cleared his throat to deflect her insult before he continued. "Please, let me introduce myself. I am Sir Weston Quinsley, the Duke of Remonnet. I am here as a Trade Emissary for the Lord of Bainbridge. My business is with the Black Thistle Castle."

"Forgive me, Sir Quinsley. I meant no disrespect."

"How could you know, Madame?"

"Let me show you to your room. You will find it simple. It will certainly lack the finery that I am sure you are accustomed, but it is clean. I will see that a tub is brought to your room. You need not bathe in the wash house with the other men."

"You are very kind, Madame."

Jario and the driver followed Bertha up the stairs to his room. As he looked around the sparsely furnished room, he found her description quite truthful. It lacked the finery he had once enjoyed, but it was clean. With the trunk set at the foot of the bed, the man made his way to the door. Opening the pouch that hung from his belt, Jario retrieved a few coins and put them in the open palm of the driver.

"If you be need'n me to be help'n you, ask for Jingles. Everyone knows me. I'll come right quick to aid you."

"Thank you Jingles. I will indeed ask. You are a good man."

Jingles gave him a clumsy bow and backed out through the doorway leaving Bertha at his side.

"Sir Quinsley, I'll be need'n payment fur the room. It is three coins fur the room and three more fur two meals a day. You can pay fur the hot water fur your tub when you call fur it, and it will cost you one more coin."

"Madame, hold out your hand."

Bertha held her hand toward him and watched as he gently shook the pouch allowing five silver coins to fall upon her open palm.

"Let me know when you expect more from me, and while I am here, please call me Quinn. It would please me if you would. There is no need to make your patrons uncomfortable."

"If you will call me Bertha instead of Madame, I surely will."

"Agreed."

"Well, I'll be leave'n you to your privacy. We'll be setting venison stew and fresh bread out this evening. I hope you will join us. It has been awhile since I have been able to look upon such a handsome face."

"It would be my honor, Bertha."

After giving him a smile, she dropped the coins between her plump bosoms and closed the door behind her. He could hear her humming as she headed down the stairs, and her merriment made him wonder what other pleasures he might find available to him as the sky darkened.

* * *

Standing on the second-floor landing, Jario could hear the laughter and banter of those gathered in the tavern. At first, the screeching sounds of their voices were painful and seemed to insult his ears. His imprisonment in the dungeon of Firelight Castle had offered him nothing but a life of utter silence, but as time went on, he soon found those familiar sounds soothed his broken mind.

As he descended the wooden stairs, the pungent smell of tobacco mixed with sweat brought back memories of drinking ale in the Echo Bluff Tavern with Buck and Gusty. That and bedding Magna had been his favorite pastime. Now, Gusty had turned against him to align with Lord Gautier, Buck had run from the island, and his lovely Magna had received her final death.

Forget the past, he thought. It offers nothing but pain and regret. I must think of the great reward that awaits me. Better yet, think of what pleasures will be mine before the morning light creeps through my window.

As he stepped from the stairs, he caught sight of a woman with long red hair and a black corset tied tightly at her back. He gasped and steadied himself with his hand upon the banister.

Could it be? Has she somehow escaped her death?

His mind flew to thoughts of Magna. Closing his eyes, he could see her sitting at her dressing table pulling pearl capped pins from her hair and letting long red strands of hair fall upon her bare creamy back.

"Have you lost yer way?" Bertha asked, as she nudged him with her hip. "Do you need help find'n a table?"

Jario's eyes flew open. He looked down at Bertha's broad smile and the large bowls of thick stew she held in her hands.

"I see that you have decided to join us," she laughed. "Find yerself a table, and I'll be bring'n you a bowl of yer own."

"I'll take that bowl and a thick slice of bread slathered with butter," replied Jario.

He made his way through the tables crowded with men enjoying their meal as well as vigorous conversation. In a dimly lit corner of the tavern, he spied an empty table. As he pulled the wooden stool out from under it, he caught sight of a man he had hoped he would never see again. Balgair sat across from a young woman, and it was obvious he was trying to comfort her. Her shoulders shook as if she were crying. Not wanting to be found staring, he averted his eyes to watch the open doorway from which Bertha would come forth with his meal.

Seeing her stride through the opening with a tray loaded with a bowl of stew, a hunk of bread coated with butter, and a tall mug of ale brought a sigh from his lips. As Bertha placed the tray on the table, he couldn't keep from looking over at Balgair. The woman had disappeared from view, and Balgair was beginning to stand. He threw a satchel over his shoulder and walked toward the door. Thankful the vampire was leaving without noticing him, he reached for the tall mug that dripped with foam. Lifting it to his mouth, he looked over its rim in hopes of seeing the vampire was gone. Instead, Balgair turned and offered him a smile before gracefully bowing. Jario sat frozen as he heard Balgair laugh before he disappeared into thin air.

"Is something wrong, sir?" asked Bertha. "You have not touched yer stew."

"Everything is fine. I thought I recognized someone I had not seen in a very long time, but I was mistaken." He picked up the hunk of bread and dipped it into the thick brown sauce of the stew before taking a bite. "It is delicious. My compliments to the cook."

Bertha was pleased with his response and hurried off to remove the dirty dishes from tables that were left empty.

After taking the last swallow of ale, Jario pushed back away from the table allowing him to lean his back against the wall. As he did, he caught the eye of a young lass watching him. Her cheeks blushed when she noticed his gaze. Hoping she would be brave enough to follow him, he stood and made his way up the stairs and down the hall to his room. As he opened the door, he saw her slowly walking toward him. He stepped into his room leaving the door open. Facing the window with his back to the door, he waited as he gazed upon the three-quarter moon through the threadbare window covering. Hearing the door close, he turned to see her standing before him. Offering her a smile, he stepped toward her.

This will be an enjoyable evening after all.

* * *

"You are up early," laughed Bertha. "I thought you might still be taken pleasure in the comforts of yer warm bed." She saw him smirk as she removed a plate from her tray that held boiled eggs, bread, sliced apples, and browned sausages. As she placed it before him, she asked, "Milk, water, or ale?"

"It is a bit early for ale. Water will do fine."

Bertha returned with a pitcher of water to see that he had nearly finished his meal.

"There is more if you be need'n it. It is simple enough to get you another plate."

"I found the meal filling enough. Might I ask you to make me another to carry with me? I am traveling to Black Thistle Castle, and I am not sure what I will find along the way."

"I will see to it."

"Oh, may I trouble you to see that a meal is taken to the young lass in my room on my account. She was sleeping when I left her. I believe she had too much ale and is suffering due to it."

"You are very generous. I will see to yer request."

Jario finished the last of his meal and called out to Bertha, "I am going to the stable to fetch a horse. I'll be back to claim the meal when I am ready to leave."

"As you wish," hollered Bertha.

The morning air brought with it a cool breeze from the sea. A few men were readying their wares within their small carts and storekeepers were busy sweeping the wooden slats in front of their doors. As he walked toward the stable, he noticed Jingles coming toward him.

"Do you be need'n help this morn'n?" he asked, as he removed his hat and bowed his head.

"You can help me choose a horse. I have a long ride ahead of me."

Jingles eagerly nodded and led the way to the stable. Once inside, Jario was disappointed to find so few horses.

"This here is the best of the lot. He has rested for two days."

Jario looked over the sable stallion. He felt his legs and along his back before a barrel-chested man entered the stable.

"You look'n or buy'n?" asked the man.

"Buy'n," replied Jario. "How much for the sable?"

"I'm a fair man. What do you offer?"

Jario had no time for bickering over a horse and opened his pouch removing three silver coins.

"You have yerself a horse, sir."

"He'll be need'n a blanket, a saddle, and reins. I'm think'n the coin he done give you to be plenty," offered Jingles with a grin.

Jario smiled at Jingles and then at the man. "I agree. What say you?"

"Take what you need," the man huffed, as he turned and left

the stable.

"You did good, Jingles. Now, ready this stallion and meet me in front of the tavern."

Chapter 6

The Encounter

The ride away from Woods Village, over Wood Cutter's Water, and past the Old Mill was uneventful. Jario had spent most of his time thinking of the young lass that had followed him to his room. She had been shy and inexperienced in the ways of satisfying men but very willing to please. It had been the sight of his fangs that required him to take the fear and pain away with a few compelling words. Her young blood tasted like sweet nectar, and he forced himself to stop when he felt her weakening heartbeat. Nearly sated, he healed the wounds he had left on her body, taken her memories, and finally allowed her to sleep. He had kissed her bare shoulder and left a coin on her pillow before heading downstairs. If his plan to retrieve the sword were successful, he would return to the tavern within a few days hoping to find her willing to share his bed again before he made his way back to the Isle of Flames.

As he crossed Whistler's River, he noticed an unusually strong scent of lavender hung in the air. He couldn't imagine where it was coming from, for he had never encountered that scent upon the island. Following the scent led him to what he had known to be the Canyon of Obscurity. Apprehensively, he neared the canyon's edge and was stunned to see the canyon floor covered in rows of lavender, the sun's reflection in crystal clear ponds, and trees covered in pink blooms.

"How can this be?" he gasped. "This was nothing but a canyon filled with darkness the last I saw of it. Whose magical power has cured its walls?"

He felt the need to take the path that led to Velsa's hidden cottage, but the task of retrieving the sword and presenting it to Mistress Violeta was his priority. Even though he needed answers, a meeting with Velsa would have to wait.

Not far from the canyon, he could see the tops of the tall trees of Black Thistle Forest. After riding through the meadow's tall sweet grass, he finally reached its edge, and the cool shade of the forest found him weary and hungry. Jumping down from his stallion, he could hear the sound of a nearby stream and made his way toward the sound to quench their thirsts. Finding a dry log next to the narrow stream, he sat down to rest. As he feasted on the meal Bertha had prepared for him, he thought more of the canyon and what might have caused it to change. He knew of the War of the Witches and the destruction it had caused, which meant someone just as powerful must have reversed the curse. Anyone wielding that kind of power was dangerous and someone he wanted to avoid.

Back on his stallion, Jario rode toward the edge of the forest. Through the trees, he caught a glimpse of a castle wall, and a shiver raced down his spine. It seemed different to him and feared the shiver he had felt might be a warning. Not to be deterred, he rode through the last of the trees and took in the full view of Black Thistle Castle. The dark clouds he remembered that hung above the castle were gone, and the sun shone brightly upon the castle's black stones. Purple thistles thrived where the withered black thistles had once surrounded the castle walls, and the moat had lost its black color.

First the canyon and now the thistles have changed. I fear what waits for me inside those castle walls could mean my death.

Suddenly, he thought of something he had completely forgotten. He hadn't given any thought to the conversation he would have as a Trade Emissary or what he could offer in trade.

Jumping from his stallion, he began to pace back and forth trying to think of something he could offer. When he had resided at Crimson Claw Castle, Claudia had often spoken of the need of spices for cooking and woven goods for bed linens. They would both easily travel, and he could guarantee they would not arrive spoiled. He knew every commander would be in need of weapons, and a large quantity of newly made swords and daggers would surely sweeten his offer.

That was easy enough. Lord Bainbridge is willing to trade spices, weapons, and woven goods for what? The only thing Alltree Island has in abundance is trees. Of course, it was obvious. Lord Bainbridge would be in need of lumber.

Satisfied with his preparedness for an emissary's conversation, he mounted his stallion and rode through the remaining trees to the clearing. It was the purple thistles that had him distracted, and he tried to ignore the fear it instilled in him.

Where are the black thistles? They were withered when I ran from the castle, but they were there. Now, I see the bright purple flowers and green stalks of common thistles. Much has changed.

"Just let me find the sword and get far away from this place," he whispered.

Confused and unsure of what or who he would find at the castle, he rode toward the drawbridge. As he cleared the gate of the castle, he was unprepared for the fear that shrouded his mind. One mistake would be all it would take to find him captured, cursed, or dead.

A guard shouted for him to halt. As he did, his reins were immediately taken from him.

"Who are you and what business have you with Black Thistle?" demanded the guard.

"I am Sir Weston Quinsley, Duke of Remonnet. I am here as the Trade Emissary for Lord Bainbridge of Hawk Perch Island. I wish to speak to your Chief Council regarding the matter of trade."

"Sir Quinsley, if you will kindly dismount, I will escort you to the Council Chamber where you will wait for Rex, the Head of the Council."

Jario dismounted and watched as a young lad led his horse away.

"Young Gordon will see that your horse is watered and ready for your departure," declared the guard.

Jario nodded as another guard approached.

"Smitz, advise Rex that Sir Quinsley is here to see him. I will escort him to the Council Chamber."

"At once," he replied, as he hurried toward the castle door.

"Follow me," the guard ordered.

Jario followed the guard through the familiar halls of the castle. He was relieved to see that little had changed within the castle walls and hoped that the sword was still safely stored in the hidden chamber. As they approached the Council Chamber, he could make out the sound of a woman's voice off in the distance and immediately knew it to be that of Lady Kayleigh. He could hear the rustle of her gown and the soft leather of her slippers moving toward them. A sense of panic flared within him just before a guard directed him through the open doorway. Once inside, the guard closed the door and offered Jario a seat. Grateful for the chair and the privacy, he sat down and tried to remember a man named Rex. The name was unfamiliar to him, but he worried he might hold some power that would recognize his disguise.

It wasn't long before the door opened and in walked a man that was large enough to fill the doorway. White hair covered his head and chin. A gold earring hung from one ear, and a thin red scar shadowed his right eyebrow. He was the spitting image of Omar, the Head of the Evergreen Council, and undoubtedly his younger brother. Relieved, Jario quickly stood.

"Sir Quinsley," Rex said, as he offered his hand in greeting. "I understand you have something to discuss with me."

"Yes, Lord Bainbridge has sent me to commission a trade alliance. He has heard of the grand forests that grow on your beautiful island and desires a few ships full of their lumber."

"Our trees offer much to this island. What would you offer in return?"

"We have an abundance of spices, the ability to produce woven goods, and our blacksmiths make the finest swords and daggers."

"Let's sit. I would like to hear more of these goods."

The discussions between Jario and Rex had gone well. Since Rex was inclined to address the trade proposal with Lord Gautier before making a final decision, it meant Jario would have to return for another meeting. After giving the guard instructions to escort Jario back to his horse, Rex asked, "Where might we send word of Lord Gautier's decision?"

Woods Village was too far to receive word quickly, and he would need to stay somewhere closer to the castle. He could go to Hunter's Point to wait, but that was too close to Crimson Claw Castle and the huge vampire, Seth. He was unsure of the powers the vampire had acquired and didn't want to risk discovery. Peak's View reeked of sheep, and he had no desire to sleep in someone's barn. Echo Bluff was familiar but out of the question. It was too close to the Evergreen Castle and the army he betrayed. The only village left was Primrose Pond. The tavern was small, but it would have to do. He had slept in worse places.

"I have taken a room at the tavern in Primrose Pond."

"Very well, I will see that word is sent to you as soon as I have Lord Gautier's answer. For now, I will take my leave and allow the guard to escort you to your horse."

As they approached the doors to the courtyard, Jario could hear the same padding of leather slippers he had heard before.

"Sir Quinsley, may I have a moment?" called Kayleigh.

He watched as Lady Kayleigh walked toward him and knew she must have spoken with Rex. He winced as he remembered their last meeting and the pain it had caused him.

"Sir Quinsley, may I present the Lady Kayleigh," announced the guard.

"Lady Kayleigh," Jario responded, as he bowed deeply before

her.

"Sir Quinsley, I am told you must return to hear Lord Gautier's decision as to your proposal for trade between our kingdoms. I am truly sorry for the delay, but to make amends, I would like to invite you to the Masquerade Ball to be held here at Black Thistle two evenings from now."

"I thank you for your apology, but it is not necessary. Matters like these take time; however, I am honored to receive your personal invitation and willingly accept."

"Wonderful, we will expect you at sundown. A mask will be made available if it is needed. Until then, I bid you a good day Sir Quinsley."

Jario bowed again and watched Lady Kayleigh turn and walk away.

Will I require an escort everywhere I go within the castle? If so, my task will be more than difficult. My only chance to retrieve the sword will be the night of the masquerade. The Great Hall full of masked people will surely keep everyone out of my way.

"Come, your horse should be ready," said the guard.

Jario followed the guard out through the open doors and down the stone steps to his horse. With reins in hand, he looked back at the wooden doors and the empty stone pedestal to their left. He remembered he had rested his hand against the stone to keep his balance after jumping through the broken doors. It had held a stone wolf. He had touched its paw, and now, it was gone. Memories flooded his mind, and he turned his stallion toward the open gate and raced for the forest. Troubled by all he had seen, he knew he had to find Velsa's cottage. He needed an explanation for all the strange things that had transpired during his absence from Alltree Island.

* * *

As Jario rode through the trees, he thought of all the times he had tried to find the witch's cottage. More often than not, Velsa had played with him until his frustration had been so great he was ready to leave. Then and only then would she reveal her cottage to him. Today, he had no patience for her games of trickery.

Further, into the forest, he rode until he came upon a small cottage that lay in ruins. The stone walls had crumbled, the glass panes of the windows lay crushed among the weeds, and the thatching appeared to have burned.

Could this be Velsa's cottage? Did someone burn the witch? Is that why the canyon is no longer dark, and the deadly thistles are no more? Had she owned the curse like the stories whispered year after year?

Troubled again by another strange sight, he turned his horse toward Primrose Pond. He needed to rest his weary mind. The small tavern would offer him a quiet room until he returned to the castle, and a few mugs of ale would wash the visions from his jumbled thoughts. While he was there, he would ask about the crumbled cottage he had seen in the forest. Surely, someone would know of its demise.

It wasn't long before he crossed the narrow end of Whistler's River and found himself near the pond where he had secretly met with Laralynn after the festival. Purely out of curiosity, he rode toward her old cottage. Approaching the weathered gate, he saw a woman kneeling in the corner of her flower garden hard at work. As she turned her head to look at him, eyes that he remembered stared back at him. He slid down from his stallion and hurried toward the vine covered fence.

"Velsa, you're alive," he blurted. "I saw what remained of your cottage and feared you were dead."

Aslev stood and stepped back away from the boisterous man.

"I know nothing of the name Velsa. My name is Aslev."

"Velsa, it is you. Aslev is the other name you often used to keep yourself hidden from others. I know it's you."

She stared at the man before her, and her mind began to ache, causing her to stumble. She pressed her fingers against her forehead trying to make the pain go away. Jario saw the look of fear in her eyes and raised his hands as he took a step back.

"Has something happened? Are you ill?"

"You have me mistaken with someone else. Please go away. Can't you see? You have made the hairs on my arms stand on end."

Jario quickly changed his appearance to allow her to see his true self. He pulled his hat down off of his head hoping to jar her memory.

"Don't you recognize me? It's Jario. Surely, you must remember me. We made a bargain to retrieve Kayleigh's tail, and I failed. I failed so badly I was cursed to a dagger that hung above Black Thistle's hearth. Velsa, don't you remember me? You always made fun of me for failing."

After seeing him change his appearance, Aslev's hands began to tremble as she backed toward her door.

"What evil is this? Stay away from me."

Feeling the handle behind her back, she pushed the door open and stepped inside.

"I do not know you. Please go away, and don't come back," Aslev shouted and closed the door.

Jario stood confused staring at her cottage door. He knew it was Velsa as sure as he knew his name, but something was terribly wrong with her. She had surely lost her mind.

Had Gautier discovered it was Velsa's plan that sent him to take the white wolf's tail and later, took her mind as revenge?

Unsure of what to do, he mounted his stallion and slowly headed for the tavern. Poor Velsa would have to wait until he had completed his task for him to help her. For now, he needed to focus his mind on the *Singing Sword.*

Chapter 7

Masquerade

The evening of the Black Thistle Masquerade Ball had finally arrived, and everyone could feel the excitement in the air. Candelabras and chandeliers full of candles were all aglow, and the light flickered against the walls like dancing fireflies. Long narrow tables covered in strips of linen cloth ran down the center of the hall. They sat dressed with bunches of lavender in pewter jugs and thistles tied with green cording hung from the backs of the chairs. In one corner, a small stage erected for the musicians and entertainers sat under an arch of wildflowers tied with colorful ribbons. It had been some time since the Great Hall filled its stone walls with music, food, and drink; and everyone at Black Thistle Castle hoped there would be many more reasons to celebrate in the future.

Gautier and Kayleigh stood just inside the open doors to the hall prepared to greet their guests. Taking Kayleigh's hand within his own, he lifted the bottom of his lion mask as he brought it to his lips and pressed a kiss to the back of her hand.

"Your mask is lovely; however, I see nothing but a mass of peacock feathers and roses made from ribbons that hide your beautiful face." He gently ran his finger over the fragile tips of a peacock plumb and raised a brow. "My dear, how many peacocks have you plucked to dress this mask and the back of your gown? Have you left them with nothing to be proud of as they strut through the meadow?"

"It was Desirae's doing. I preferred a little magic since I couldn't bear to take their beautiful feathers from them."

"If I had not seen you dress in our bedchamber this evening, I would not know you to be the lady of this castle."

"My love, is that not the meaning of masquerade? As we stand here to greet our guests, everyone will know us, and we will be forced to guess their identities. I say we should surprise our guests and let them enter on their own accord."

"If it is your desire to play this wicked game, we shall hurry away and make our entrance as everyone else will this evening."

"It shall be great fun."

As they hurried to the far end of the hall, Gautier and Kayleigh could hear the guests were beginning to arrive through the front gate.

"Gautier, make haste before someone sees us."

As the guests made their way past the open doors of the Great Hall, they were greeted only by the beauty of the decorated hall and the gentle sound of string instruments. Servants walked about offering sweet wine and ale to everyone that entered. The long tables displayed dried fruit, a variety of cheeses, and freshly baked bread. Large platters of roasted lamb, duck, and venison sat among platters filled with roasted carrots, onions, and mushrooms. To everyone's delight, several large trays of delicate sweets sat at the end of each table.

It was Oliver that managed to devour one of the sweet delicacies filled with cream before Astra could pull him away from the tempting morsels.

"Sweets are meant for tantalizing your tongue after you have dined," Astra informed him before smacking his hand as he reached for another.

"What can I say? I find sweets are my downfall. After all, I am lucky enough to have the sweetest morsel on my arm this evening."

Astra could feel her face blush and took satisfaction in

knowing that no one could see her face through her fairy mask.

"Besides, no one will know who I am in this disguise. I'm surprised you made me wear the mask of a red fox. I thought I was more like a ferocious bear."

He was suddenly interrupted by the firm grip of someone's hand upon his shoulder.

"Oliver, is that you?" asked Baxter. "You come masked as a sly fox? I thought you more like a bear than a fox. Your size is certainly that of a bear."

Oliver sighed as he looked over his shoulder at the mask of a red dragon and a woman standing beside him wearing a shimmering gown with a mask covered in sand, pearls, and shells.

"Yes, as did I, but Astra had other ideas. What gave me away?" he asked.

"Well, you are about the biggest man in the hall with the tiniest woman on your arm," he laughed. "I doubt you will fool too many of the guests."

Feeling her face blush again, Astra turned her attention to Laralynn.

"Lady Laralynn, you look lovely," offered Astra as she curtsied. "I see you have chosen the sand and the sea for your mask."

Laralynn bent down and took Astra's hands in her own. "Astra, you'll give me away," she laughed. "Yes, I have a fondness for the sea, but you have chosen a beautiful fairy. The costume suits you. Your mask reminds me of the story told to me at the Festival of the Ribbons. It was about a fairy that gives a lost girl ribbons to find her way home."

"Do they still tell that old story in Primrose Pond?" asked Astra.

"It is repeated every year during the festival to all the children. I learned about it from my friends Nollie and Lettie when I attended the festival for the first time."

"Did you know they visit Velsa quite often? I'm sorry. I mean to say Aslev."

"I do, and I am very happy that they have shown her such kindness."

"It seems to please her. She speaks of them often."

"Laralynn, I see that your mother and father have arrived," whispered Baxter.

Laralynn looked toward the entrance and saw her mother dressed in a red gown with a mask full of red and orange feathers that stood well above her forehead. By her mother's side, her father stood handsomely dressed in black and wearing a simple black mask edged in red.

"What are they?" asked Oliver.

"My mother is fire, and my father is burning embers," replied Laralynn. "Oh, I see my uncle and Gavenia have arrived and come as the white hawk and the hunter."

"Come, let's all say hello."

Taking Baxter's hand, they made their way to her mother's side.

"Mother, Father, you look quite handsome this evening."

"As do you, daughter," Thomas replied.

"My dear, have you seen Lord Gautier or Lady Kayleigh?" asked Lara.

"I was surprised they were not at the door when we arrived. I assume our hosts have hidden themselves among this masked crowd and are awaiting to be discovered."

"Brother, will you join me and leave the ladies to their discoveries?" asked Tate. "I find my thirst for ale is much more intriguing than the mysteries of what lies beneath each and every mask."

"Lead the way. I find I have already had my fill of feathers and ribbons," he replied.

"I think I will join you," laughed Baxter. "If I tarry too long, Laralynn will have me dancing the night away."

"I suspect you will come running when you find me dancing with some masked stranger," teased Laralynn. "I hear dragons can be quite protective and jealous creatures."

"Jealous and deadly to be sure . . . it might be good to

remember I have a fiery spirit."

"One I've seen quite often, too."

The men laughed as they walked away happy to be free of what was sure to be conversations filled with gossip. It wasn't long before they each stood satisfied with a mug of ale clutched in their hands.

* * *

After receiving word the next day that Lord Gautier had approved the trade alliance and meeting with Rex to sign the agreement, Jario felt more comfortable about returning to Black Thistle. He had visited the castle twice and avoided discovery. Even though escorted both times, it gave him a chance to study the grounds and the guards that patrolled its walls before he would return to attend the masquerade ball.

As Jario rode across the drawbridge and through the open gate, an odd sense of sadness and regret returned to stiffen his shoulders. As hard as he tried to forget, he still missed its stone walls. Clenching his teeth, he forced his memories from his mind and focused on the task before him. There was no plot forced upon him as Velsa had done. He was here to retrieve the *Singing Sword* for the Mistress Violeta and nothing more.

"Sir, may I take yer horse?" asked the young lad he had seen twice before. "I'll be keep'n him safe. You have me word."

Jario dismounted and handed the reins of his horse to the young lad. Opening a burlap bag that hung from the horn of the saddle, he withdrew a white mask full of antlers.

Looking down at the lad's fearful stare, he laughed, "It is the mask of a white stag, not a demon. You may touch it if you like. It can do you no harm."

He held it out for the lad and watched him run his finger along an antler. Seeing the lad was satisfied, he lifted it over his head and pulled it down over his face.

"See that he has fresh water and keep him near. I may not stay long. I'll need him ready at the gate."

The lad nodded his head and led the horse away.

Remember who you have become, he thought. One little mistake and you'll find yourself cursed back inside a dagger hanging on Gautier's wall again for eternity or possibly worse.

As Jario entered the familiar Great Hall, he took in the crowd and their whimsical disguises. There was an abundance of feathers and ribbons adorning each and every woman's face, while the men wore masks of forest animals and magical creatures. It was the overwhelming number of red gowns that caught his attention and made him think of Magna. He knew she would have loved hiding behind a mask and taking some poor unsuspecting soul to the dungeon for an evening of wicked games. Surprised by the lump in his throat, he made his way into the crowd. Taking a goblet from the first tray offered him, he attempted to drown his sorrow.

Jario noticed the doors at the far end of the hall had been left open and seeing they were left unguarded pleased him. It would be his easiest path to the hidden chamber, but a path used mainly by servants. He would have to maneuver the hallway using his haze to remain undetected, or face capture. The mask and image of Sir Weston Quinsley would only hide him momentarily if discovered by Lord Gautier or Desirae. Their powers would surely be able to see through his disguise and possibly his haze.

The music began to play, and several couples moved quickly to claim their space for dancing. It had been some time since Jario had danced, and he was fascinated with the way the women swirled around the men, their bodies nearly touching their partners. Standing with a goblet of sweet wine in one hand, he studied the intricate steps the men performed so easily. He was so enthralled by what he saw that he carelessly stepped back into the woman standing behind him. Turning to apologize, he quickly bowed and saw a white feather drift toward the floor.

"Forgive me, My Lady," he said, as he politely bowed and then retrieved the feather that had landed across the toe of his boot. "Sir Weston Quinsley at your service, I meant you no harm."

The memory of a white feather took him back to his bedchamber where his beautiful white hawk had perched on the post of his bed.

The woman curtsied and then replied, "I am Gavenia, and you have caused me none."

Jario knew that name. She was the woman he and Magna had tortured in the dungeon, and that meant Tate would be near. With Tate came danger, and he wanted none of it. He needed to step away, for if discovered, his arrest would be inevitable.

"I see I have ruined the back of your gown."

"It is merely a single feather, Sir Quinsley. There is no damage and nothing to forgive."

"Then I shall keep it as a memento of our meeting, My Lady. Enjoy the ball."

Gavenia smiled and nodded. Hearing Tate's voice, she turned to find him. When she turned back around, Sir Quinsley had vanished.

Jario had pulled his haze to hide from her and possibly from Tate. Walking to a dark corner, he made sure no one was looking his way and released his haze. Stepping back into the light, he reached for another goblet of sweet wine from a servant's tray and downed it before making his way back into the crowd. He knew he was running out of time. The longer he remained in the castle, the bigger the risk of being caught. If he didn't retrieve the sword while he had this brief freedom, he would have to steal his way inside using his haze and risk certain discovery in Gautier's bedchamber.

With his mind made up, he sat his empty goblet on the corner of a table and headed for the open doors to the hallway. He had only gone a few steps when he was surprised to find a familiar scent that caused him to halt. He searched the masks for the one that called to him. Moving toward a gathering of women, the scent of lemon and mint grew stronger. A woman wearing a red gown and a feathered mask laughed, and he felt a yearning he had long forgotten. It was the sweet laugh of Lady Lara. Seeing the young woman beside her, he was sure it was her daughter, Lady Laralynn.

You fool, stay away from them. Stay true to your task. Haven't you learned anything from your failures? The Evergreen women have been nothing but trouble.

"Sir Quinsley," a voice called to him.

Jario looked up to see Gavenia standing beside Lady Lara.

"Come meet Lady Lara and Lady Laralynn."

Reluctantly, Jario made his way to Gavenia's side.

"Sir Quinsley, I was just telling Lady Lara of our earlier meeting. Lady Lara, this is Sir Weston Quinsley."

Jario bowed and kissed the back of her hand. As he inhaled her scent, it was all he could do to keep his fangs from descending.

"It is an honor to meet you. I am at your service, My Lady."

"And, this is Lady Laralynn, her daughter."

"My Lady," he said, as he bowed and kissed the back of her hand. "It is an honor to meet you."

"You are new to Alltree Island, Sir Quinsley. Have you much business here on the island?" asked Lara.

Remember she can read minds, he thought. You must clear your mind of all thoughts of her.

"Yes, I am the Trade Emissary for Lord Bainbridge, and I have just signed an agreement with Lord Gautier."

"Where are you from?" asked Laralynn.

"I sailed here from Hawk Perch Island."

"I would love to sail away to someplace new," Laralynn said, as she motioned with her hand spilling sweet wine upon the sleeve of his tunic. Embarrassed, she quickly began brushing the wine away.

"I'm very sorry. I have spoiled your tunic."

"It is of no consequence, My Lady."

The music began to play, and he saw Laralynn's eyes brighten.

"I see you are an admirer of music."

"And dancing," she replied.

"Would you honor me with a dance?"

"It is the least I can do to make up for spoiling your tunic, but I must warn you. A dragon could interrupt us at any moment. He claims merely to be protective, but I believe him to be a jealous dragon."

"I shall heed your warning. I fear I am no match for the fiery breath of a dragon. I have left my shield behind."

"If you are still willing, Sir Quinsley, I will take your hand and dare the mighty dragon to intervene."

Jario laughed and held out his hand. He felt Laralynn place her hand upon his as they made their way toward the others that were dancing. Facing each other, they moved in step to the music while weaving around couples. As they held hands to scurry under an arch made by couples holding hands above their heads, he heard her laugh. It reminded him of the moments they had spent at the pond and his painful failure.

I need to get on with my task.

The music stopped, and he led Laralynn back to her mother's side.

"Sir Quinsley, thank you for the dance."

Taking Laralynn's hand, he kissed it lightly and said, "It was my pleasure; however, if you will excuse me, I need to find Lord Gautier and Lady Kayleigh to thank them for this evening's invitation. Gavenia, Lady Lara, I bid you a good evening."

Laralynn smiled and watched him walk into the crowd.

* * *

Jario gradually made his way back towards the open doors that led to the dimly lit hallway. Stepping into the shadows, he quickly pulled his haze and hurried toward the stone steps that would lead him toward Gautier's bedchamber door. Taking them as rapidly and quietly as he could, he found himself staring at the large wooden door he had opened so many times. Rapping twice, he stepped back and waited for the door to open. After a few moments, he released a sigh of relief when silence was his only greeting.

As he cautiously opened the door, the light from several burning candles offered him a clear view of the bedchamber he had once called his own. To make sure he was alone, he called out again but heard no reply. Satisfied, he stepped into the bedchamber. After closing the door behind him, he removed his mask and tossed it on a bench beside the door. A sudden wave of memories bombarded his mind, and he heard the foreign words Gautier had chanted as he stood naked before him. For a moment, he felt the pain from the flames that had consumed his body, and he forced himself to keep from crying out. The room began to spin causing him to stumble, and with one hand pressed against his forehead, he reached for the back of a chair to keep from falling.

"Begone, I have no time for tricks of the mind. You must leave me in peace."

Looking up, he saw the doors to the balcony had been left open, and he reveled in the cool breeze that brushed against his face. Moving his hand to his chest, he concentrated on the medallion and hoped it would chase the visions away. A sudden feeling of calmness began to weave through his body.

"It appears the medallion is good for something, after all."

Making his way to the wall, he quickly found the small stone that was set deep into the stone floor and pressed it firmly with the sole of his boot. The deep groan of the panel as it swung toward him was music to his ears, and he smiled as he watched the light wash across the dark chamber's stone floor beckoning him forward. Without hesitation, he entered the chamber to find it was nearly the same. The wooden chests still sat upon the thick shelves, but the books and parchments were gone. He surmised they had been taken by Lady Kayleigh to the library, for he had seen her there among the books before Lord Gautier had cursed him to the dagger.

Letting his eyes scan the longswords and daggers that hung on the wall, he searched for the simple sword that would be his journey's prize. Panic caused his fangs to descend when he discovered it no longer hung on the wall. He madly began searching the chamber for the missing sword. He was about to give up when he noticed a bundle of linen lying in the shadows beneath a table. Bending down, he retrieved the bundle and unrolled its end to find the gleam of a sword's blade. Pulling it free from its covering, he saw a single ruby and the leather bindings of its hilt. Turning the blade over in his hands, he held it up to the light and saw the engraving of *Fuaim na Cumhacta* and knew he had found the *Singing Sword*. As he ran his fingers over the words, he heard the humming sound he had heard once before; however, this time, it was only a sweet melody and nothing more.

After rewrapping the sword, he ran his free hand over the stone wall in search of the one stone that would close the panel. Finding it, he pressed the heel of his hand against it and quickly exited the chamber as the panel began to groan. With sword and mask in hand, he turned to look back one last time at the closed panel before he hurried from the bedchamber to make his leave from Black Thistle.

As he stepped from the castle into the night air, he was startled to find Lady Laralynn and Baxter in an affectionate embrace on the castle steps. Taking satisfaction in the safety of his gift of haze, he quickly made his way around them. He felt the slightest brush of Baxter's arm against his own but paid it no mind. Seeing the same young lad holding the reins of several horses, he maneuvered his body to hide among them. After releasing his haze, he stepped forward and secured his prize to the back of his saddle. Seeing the young lad's fascination with his mask, he set it down at his feet. Taking a coin from his pouch, he pressed it to the palm of the lad's small hand and took the reins. He glanced one last time at Lady Laralynn before mounting his stallion and riding through the open gate.

Jario raced from the castle toward the Black Thistle Forest. Everything had gone just as he had planned. He had retrieved the *Singing Sword* without being caught, and he could return to the Isle of Flames to place it at Mistress Violeta's feet. With his task complete, he would be able to claim the reward she had promised him.

As he wove through the thick forest, he thought again of Velsa. Something had happened to her, and he had to find out what or who had caused it. He would visit her cottage in the morning, for now, he would return to the Primrose Tavern. He had much to celebrate.

Chapter 8

Discovery

Baxter stood outside on the stone steps waiting for Laralynn. He had had his fill of music, dancing, and the lively voices in the Great Hall and was ready to return to Evergreen. It was the calm and the quiet of the night that called to him. More than anything, he looked forward to spending the rest of the evening with his arms wrapped around her as they gazed up at the stars. He often thought about what it would be like to have her in his arms every night but hadn't found the courage to ask her to be his. The ring he had commissioned was in the pouch tied at his waist, her parents had given their blessings, but he hadn't found the perfect moment to propose.

You fool, why are you waiting? I'll do it tonight. I'll ask her tonight as we stand in the dark under a canopy of twinkling stars. I'll do it tonight, and we will be wed before the next full moon.

"I have offered our appreciation and goodnights to everyone," Laralynn said, as she reached for his hand. "We have no one to bother us for the rest of the evening."

He gently removed her mask and wiped a bit of sand from her cheek with his thumb. As he leaned in to kiss her, he felt something brush against his arm. Stepping back, he looked over his shoulder to see who had made their way past them without offering their pardon. He was surprised to find no one.

"What's wrong?"

"I thought I felt something brush against my arm. It's nothing."

Laralynn looked beyond Baxter and saw the translucent image of a man walking toward a few tethered horses and gasped.

"What's wrong?"

"I thought I saw a man at first, but I can see right through him. It couldn't possibly be a man. Could he be from the Otherworld? Could he be a ghost?"

"Where is he? I don't see anyone."

"He is standing near the horses holding a mask . . . my stars, it's the mask that Sir Quinsley wore this evening."

"I still don't see anyone."

She watched as the translucent image stepped behind the cover of the horses and then reappeared transformed as Sir Quinsley.

"Over there," she pointed. "Do you see him now? Sir Quinsley must be immortal."

"He is obviously set to leave. Why would he need to hide behind his haze?"

"To hide from someone is the obvious answer."

"From who? Wait, you can see someone that has used the gift of haze?"

"It appears that I can, but more importantly, we need to find out who he is hiding from and why?"

"I have a feeling we aren't going to like the answer."

Laralynn watched as Sir Quinsley secured a bundle to his saddle and set his mask of antlers at a young lad's feet. After pressing something into the lad's palm, he took the reins held out to him, mounted his stallion, and turned him toward the gate.

"Laralynn, look at your hand."

A faint outline of a red flame covered the back of her hand. They both knew what that meant. Someone had lied to her.

"Who held your hand?"

"Several people held my hand. I was greeted by so many this evening."

"Who was the last person to hold your hand?"

"You were the last, Baxter."

"You know that I wouldn't lie to you. Think, who touched your hand before I did."

"I said goodbye to Lady Kayleigh, and Lord Gautier kissed my hand. Before that, my uncle held my hand while I said good-bye to Gavenia."

"Lord Gautier or Tate would have noticed if a bright red flame was on your hand. It had to have happened before you said your goodbyes to allow it time to fade. Who did you meet that you didn't know?"

"Sir Quinsley was the only one. I knew everyone else, but he was invited by Lady Kayleigh. He is the Trade Emissary for Lord Bainbridge from Hawk Perch Island."

"Is he? For all we know, he could be pretending to be Sir Quinsley."

"Why would he pretend to be an emissary?"

"It would be an easy way to gain access to Black Thistle Castle."

"We need to tell Lord Gautier what we have discovered."

Taking Laralynn's hand, Baxter led her back into the castle to find Lord Gautier.

"He won't be hard to find since he is one of the tallest men in the hall, and the only man wearing the mask of a lion with a peacock by his side," laughed Laralynn.

As they entered the Grand Hall, Baxter spotted Lady Kayleigh and Desirae walking toward them.

"We were just going out for a bit of air," offered Kayleigh. "Would you like to join us?"

"My Lady, we just came in to find you and Lord Gautier. The Lady Laralynn has discovered something that we feel should be brought to his attention. It could mean nothing, but at the very least, it was odd," Baxter said.

"If it concerns you enough to question it, it deserves

discussing with Gautier," replied Kayleigh. "Find him and meet us in the library. There is no need to worry our guests."

Baxter went in search of Gautier while the ladies casually made their way out of the Grand Hall. He found him in the corner speaking with Lady Lara and Lord Thomas.

"My Lady, My Lords, I have a matter that I would like to discuss with all of you," Baxter softly said, as he looked over his shoulder to see if anyone was near. "Lady Laralynn has discovered something quite unusual. Lady Kayleigh, Desirae, and the Lady Laralynn have gone to the library to wait for us."

"Very well," Gautier replied. "Take Lady Lara to the library. I will bring Thomas."

Baxter nodded and offered Lady Lara his arm, "Let's see if we can find the Lady Laralynn."

"Thomas, would you like to see the new stallion that arrived yesterday? He is a real beauty," bragged Gautier, loud enough for a few guests to hear him. "I'm sure my guests can do without me for a while."

With goblets in hand, the two men made their way through the crowd and toward the open doorway. As they passed Tate, Thomas called out to him, "Come with us brother. Lord Gautier has a new stallion he wants to show us."

Tate fell in behind his brother and followed them through the hallway. As they made the turn toward the library, they could see Killian standing outside the doorway.

"What are you doing here?" asked Gautier. "You should be with Alicia. The celebration is for both of you."

"I am the Lady Kayleigh's guardian. Even during a celebration, I watch over her. I could tell that something was wrong, and I followed her to make sure there was no danger. Apparently, my concern was not misplaced. What has happened?" asked Killian.

"We are about to find out," replied Gautier. "Step inside and close the door." With the door closed, Killian took his place next to the door, and Gautier stepped to the head of the table. "Now, who is going to tell me the reason for your concern?"

"My Lord, Baxter and I were outside on the stone steps, and I saw someone leave the castle. At first, I wasn't sure what my eyes had seen, for I thought it was a ghost. I could see right through him. He was carrying a mask as he walked toward a group of horses that were minded by a lad. He stepped behind the horses, and I lost sight of him. Suddenly, Sir Quinsley stepped from the horses and secured a bundle to his saddle. I saw him set his mask at the lad's feet and press something into the lad's hand; I believe it was a coin. He mounted his stallion and rode through the open gate."

"She saw Sir Quinsley walking from the castle covered in haze," Baxter said. "At first, I was taken aback by her new ability, but then it seemed strange that a man that had been invited to a masquerade ball would have the need to hide behind a gift of haze as he left the castle. Why would he do that?"

"If he had something to hide," muttered Thomas.

"Desirae, can you find Sir Quinsley's essence?" asked Gautier.

"It may take some time. The hall is full of people," she replied.

"He danced with me. Could his essence still be on my hands or arms?" asked Laralynn.

"Yes, I should be able to extract it from you," sighed Desirae. This will be much easier than searching an entire hall."

"Laralynn tells us he secured a bundle to his saddle. That means he was someplace other than the Grand Hall. I need to know where he has been and what was in that bundle," declared Gautier. "I believe we are searching for a thief that was pretending to be an emissary."

"I'll stay with Desirae and Laralynn," Lara said. "You should all get back to the guests."

"I'll stay too," Kayleigh said. "The people will not think anything of four women returning together. Let the men return to the hall without us."

"If Lady Kayleigh stays, I will stay," declared Killian.

"Killian, keep a watchful eye on them," ordered Gautier.

As the men left for the hall, Killian took his place beside the open doorway of the library.

Desirae lifted her skirt and pulled a small blade from a sheath bound by a narrow strip of leather at the top of her black lace stocking. After letting her skirt fall, she opened her palm and ordered Laralynn to do the same. With the point of the blade resting on her palm, Desirae whispered a few words in a language Laralynn had never heard and quickly pierced her skin. Blood began to fill her palm and dripped from between her fingers onto Laralynn's open palm.

"Laralynn, close your hand and keep it closed," ordered Desirae. "Let's see what evil essence has been left behind."

Lady Lara and Lady Kayleigh watched as mist slowly seeped from Laralynn's arms, cheek, and back in shades of blue, green, and pink. Desirae waved her hand, and they faded away.

"You were touched by many friendly souls this evening," sighed Desirae. "You are loved by many."

Laralynn felt a shiver race up her back, and her hand began to shake.

"Don't open your hand," insisted Desirae. "The evil essence is trying to stay hidden within your body."

"My hand is burning," cried Laralynn. "I can't keep it closed much longer."

It took only a moment more for the evil essence to appear. Its black mist clung to Laralynn's arm and the small of her back as if it owned her. As it began swirling around her body, the burning sensation stopped.

"Laralynn, open your hand, now," demanded Desirae.

As she did, the mist began circling her arm and slithering toward her palm like a snake. Drawn by the scent of blood, it was slowly consumed as it dared to taste the blood of Desirae's trap.

"Close your hand, and don't open it until I give the order."

Desirae waved her hands over Laralynn's fist. Red sparks flew from her fingertips as she began muttering, "Obey my request, you must find the path of your master."

Laralynn could feel the burning sensation returning and felt tears welling in her eyes.

"Throw the blood to the floor. Laralynn, you must throw it to the floor, now."

Laralynn threw the blood from her hand toward the stone floor. As it hit the stones, the black mist returned and swirled up to the ceiling. She backed away as she saw it begin to take the form of a man. There were no identifiable features, other than, the shape of a mask with antlers."

"It's him," gasped Laralynn. "It's Sir Quinsley."

"Do as I have commanded, find the path of your master," snapped Desirae.

The misty image turned toward Desirae and raised an arm in defiance.

"I have commanded you to find the path of your master," she snapped. "I will not ask again."

After lowering its arm, it turned and drifted toward Killian. Never stopping, it passed through his body and out into the hallway.

"What was that?" gasped Killian. "Even my wolf felt it."

"We believe it to be the essence of Sir Quinsley," replied Desirae. "Stay close while we follow it."

Killian kept his hand on his dagger as he followed the women through the hallway. As they approached the Grand Hall, everyone adjusted their masks and entered as if nothing had been amiss. Keeping their eyes on the image, they watched it circle around the guests and then drift toward the open doors at the far end of the hall.

"That doorway leads to the steps for the second floor. It is where our personal quarters are located," whispered Kayleigh.

Lara reached out to Thomas' mind, *Thomas, we are following the essence of Sir Quinsley, and it is near the open doors at the far end of the hall. I think it best that you come with us. Kayleigh believes it is heading toward their personal quarters.*

Without hesitation, the image drifted up the stone steps and along the dimly lit hallway until it reached a set of carved wooden doors. It paused for a moment, and then passed through the doors. Kayleigh quickly opened the door, and Desirae followed her into the bedchamber. One moment later and they would have missed the image passing through the wood-paneled wall.

By now, Gautier had made his way into the bedchamber and reached for Kayleigh's hand. Killian stayed in the hallway to keep watch while Thomas and Baxter entered to find everyone staring at the wall.

"Gautier, what is behind this wall?" asked Desirae.

"A hidden chamber," he replied. "It once held books and maps until Kayleigh moved them to the library. Now, old daggers and swords hang on the walls, and I keep chests filled with coins behind the safety of this wall."

"The image we followed passed through this wall. I need you to open it and tell me if anything is missing."

Gautier stepped toward the wall and pressed the toe of his boot against a small stone that protruded from the floor. The wall groaned as it swung into the bedchamber revealing a small dark chamber. He removed a burning torch from a bracket on the wall and made his way inside. Raising the lid of each chest, he found each chest still full of coins. He saw that the jeweled daggers and swords still lined the walls. Turning to Desirae, he shook his head, "I find that nothing is missing."

Seeing the swords and daggers hanging on the walls, Laralynn's mind drifts to the story of the curse against Violeta and her need for the *Singing Sword*. She steps into the small chamber and asks, "Lord Gautier, do you know of the *Singing Sword*?"

Gautier searched his mind, but it was clouded with the dark, painful memories of the years he had spent locked away from Kayleigh. Pushing the darkness aside, he recalled the sound a sword made when his father ran his finger over the blade.

"I seem to recall a sword my father had secured to the wall. It had been a gift from my father to my brother, Gerwig. When he ran his finger over the blade, it made a humming sound. There were words engraved on the blade, *Fuaim na Cumhacta,*" he replied. "I know the words to mean *Sound of Power*, but it was an old sword. Others may have called it the *Singing Sword.*"

"Does it still hang on the wall?" asked Laralynn.

Gautier looked about the chamber but found nothing resembling the sword.

"I noticed it had fallen to the floor," offered Kayleigh. "I wrapped it in cloth and placed it under the table for safekeeping until the brace could be repaired." She looked where she had put the sword and found the floor bare. "It is gone."

"Mother, do you not think this odd?" asked Laralynn. "Meadow tells us that Jario is coming to Alltree Island and a story about the Mistress Violeta needing a *Singing Sword*. A stranger by the name of Sir Quinsley arrives seeking a trade agreement with Black Thistle Castle. I see him covered in his gift of haze as he leaves the castle carrying a bundle."

"A bundle that is missing from Lord Gautier's chamber," added Baxter. "We know that Jario has the gift of haze."

"He has the power to change his appearance, thanks to me, and he knew of the hidden chamber," moaned Gautier. "We have been outsmarted by more of Jario's evil ways. I am sure he has stolen the *Singing Sword.*"

"As a traitor of Evergreen Castle, he has avoided arrest for too long," declared Thomas. "Evergreen's Army will block his escape from the harbors. He will be arrested and feel the wrath of a traitor's death. I think it best we return to Evergreen and quickly set a plan in order before he can leave this island."

"Thomas, promise me that I will see him one last time before his final death?" asked Gautier. "I owe him much for his attack on my beloved Kayleigh and Killian, her guardian."

"I will, my friend."

Chapter 9

The Chase

The Evergreen Command Center was buzzing with excitement over the possibility of finally arresting the traitor. It was clear that Jario's goal had been to steal the *Singing Sword* for Mistress Violeta and return to the Isle of Flames. To do that, he had to board a ship. Commander Preston had put together a plan to counter his actions, and Lord Thomas had firmly issued the orders.

Elda and Oliver would patrol and guard the village of Echo Bluff and its harbor. The southern harbor of the island, Cobb Cove, and the village of Peaks View would be guarded by Tate, while Gavenia's hawk would patrol the Black Thistle Forest by air.

Baxter would be charged with warning Astra to keep watch over her sister, Aslev. It was feared that Jario would try to seek out help from his old friend. If she didn't comply, he might harm her or worse. Baxter would then make his way through Primrose Pond and Shepard's Grove before going on to patrol Woods Village and guard Woods Bay.

Lord Gautier had sent word that Desirae would make a visit to Crimson Claw Castle to warn Seth of Jario's return to the island. It was unlikely he would request assistance from the giant vampire, but if he was desperate, he might attempt a bargain with the vampire to save his life.

Woodward had been sent to the aviary to prepare the message hawks for flight. It would merely be a courtesy to warn Fallon and Cumberland Castles, for it was doubtful that Jario would attempt to find sanctuary where he had taken great delight in spoiling both of the lord's only daughters.

With nothing left to do but ready their weapons and their horses, they would leave at first light. There was only one problem with the plan. Laralynn had been ordered to stay at Evergreen, and she was furious with her father.

Laralynn rapped on her parent's bedchamber door and waited. She could hear her mother scolding her father, and she took great pleasure in it. Hearing the bolt drawn back, she held her breath hoping to see her mother. The door opened wide, and her mother greeted her with a knowing smile.

"Come in, I was expecting your visit. Your father and I were talking about his decision."

Laralynn entered the bedchamber and found her father facing the hearth. He stood with his arms crossed over his chest staring at the flames.

"Father, I need to speak to you and mother about my role in searching for Jario."

"Were my orders not clear enough for you? Must I repeat them?"

"They were clear, but I feel I can help. I know I can make a difference. I am here to try and make you understand how I can be valuable to the plan."

Thomas spun around and faced his daughter.

"Do you not understand how valuable you are to me? I could not bear it if something happened to you. Jario has shown a fascination for you and your mother, and I need to keep you both far away from him."

"Father, my place is with the army."

"Listen to her, Thomas."

"I know this pains you, but I took an oath like every other member of the army. It is my duty to defend Evergreen from

Jario or anyone else that wishes us harm."

"Laralynn, I cannot lose you."

"Can you bear to lose their lives? Why is my life more important than theirs?"

"Your life is more important to me because you are my daughter and I love you."

Laralynn rushed into her father's arms and felt the comfort of his warm embrace. It was the sound of his weeping that stilled her heart, and she pushed back to look at his face.

"Father, I know I can help capture Jario. He will think he can hide from the army by using his gift of haze; however, he is unaware that I have the gift to see through the haze. No one else can do that. We can use that gift to our advantage. Please, give me this chance to prove my worth to the army and to you."

Thomas looked at Lara hoping she would come to his aid and deny his daughter's request, but she stood silent. It was then that he heard her voice in his mind.

"I remember a time that you were told by Tate to stay behind for your own safety. You did not listen and endeavored the Canyon of Obscurity on your own to save me. Laralynn is like her father. She is stubborn and has your courage. My love, grant her request."

It was true. Everything Lara had said was true.

"Laralynn, your mother has reminded me of a time when I faced a similar situation. By doing so, she has lightened my burden. Therefore, I will grant your request on one condition. You will be paired with Baxter and follow his orders. Do you understand?"

"Yes, I understand, thank you. You have made me so happy," she said, as she snuggled into her father's embrace.

"Now, kiss your mother. There is little time before the search begins."

Laralynn did as her father asked and hurried from their bedchamber eager to find Baxter.

* * *

Jario had found the spirited lass behind the stable cleaning mud from a rider's boots. The few coins she would collect from her chore would pay for a warm stall filled with fresh hay and a place to sleep for the night. After offering her a meal in exchange for her company, she eagerly washed the mud from her hands and followed him into the tavern.

He had bought them both a bowl of stew and two wedges of bread slathered with butter. Once it was set before her, she offered him little conversation until the bowl was empty. Eyeing the men playing darts, she had begged him to play. He succumbed to her wish and let her win until she had tired of the game. It made no difference to him who had won the game. He had already won the game of seduction and was ready to receive his prize.

He woke to the feel of something tickling his nose. He tried to brush it away and discovered a mass of red curly hair sprawled across his chest. The young lass draped over his body had spent most of the evening celebrating her good fortune with a meal to warm her belly. He had celebrated with the taste of her blood.

Lifting her by the shoulder, he gently rolled her over trying not to wake her. Once free of the lass, he slowly sat up and put both feet on the floor. As he rubbed the sleep from his eyes, he thought of Velsa, again. Her reaction to him had left him feeling unsettled. Someone or something had meddled with her mind, and he needed to know who was to blame. He decided to allow himself one more visit, and then, he would make his way to the harbor.

Dressed and eager to be on his way, Jario knelt beside the bed. He reached his hand under the wooden frame and retrieved his precious bundle. Tucking it under his arm, he stood and glanced one last time at the sleeping lass. She had played his games, and her smile had reminded him of a woman that was lost to him. Shaking the painful vision from his mind, he pulled a silver coin from his pouch and placed it between her breasts. It caused her to stir, and as she reached for the warmth of the coverlet, he hurried from the room.

* * *

The sight of the thatched roof of her cottage and the smoke that drifted from its stack meant he was almost there. He had reluctantly released Sir Quinsley's appearance long before he reached the empty dirt road but assured himself she would remember his true appearance. After all, she had always known when he was near and loved to make a teasing game of it.

As he approached the thicket of blooming morning glories, he could see Velsa kneeling with her back to him in a patch of freshly turned soil. Certain that she had heard the clomping hooves, he watched her stand and turn toward him. A bright smile covered her face but quickly turned to concern.

"It is good to see you," called Jario from atop his stallion. "I brought you a fresh bun stuffed with sage and sausage. It is from the tavern in Primrose Pond."

He saw her lick the corner of her mouth as she watched him unwrap the cloth that covered the freshly baked bun.

"I'm going to slide from my saddle and meet you at the gate."

She didn't offer a response, but he thought it good that she didn't back away.

Standing beside his stallion, he held his cloth draped hand out toward her as he slowly walked toward the gate. She matched him step for step; until, they stood face to face.

"It's for you, and I think it is still slightly warm."

She wiped her hands on her apron and carefully removed the golden-brown morsel from the cloth. Tearing it in half, she handed a portion back to Jario. He accepted her gift and took a bite. She did the same.

Jario heard the door to the cottage open, and a young fair-haired woman stepped out into the sunlight.

"Aslev, who visits you?" asked Astra.

"A man brought me a sausage bun. It is quite tasty," replied

Aslev.

"Aslev, step back away from the man. I have told you not to speak to strangers."

"I knew her once. It was when the canyon still held the darkness, and she lived in a cottage within the Black Thistle Forest," he explained, hoping she would return to the cottage.

"Aslev, come back into the cottage. I feel danger surrounds this man."

As Aslev started to turn toward Astra, Jario grabbed her arm to make her stay. A shrieking sound left her mouth, none of which, Jario had ever heard. Purple sparks flew from her fingers, and he felt pain shoot from his hands up his arms. He released her arm and looked down at the burns on the palms of his hands. When he looked back up, he found her sitting on the roof of the cottage.

"Off with you!" screamed Astra. "See what you have done."

Jario had seen enough. The witch had surely gone mad. He ran to his stallion and heaved himself up onto his saddle. Without looking back, he raced toward the road that would take him to Woods Bay and the *Withering Rose*.

* * *

As Baxter and Laralynn rode from the trees, the first thing she saw was Aslev standing on the roof of her cottage, and then Astra standing in the middle of the garden trying to coax her down.

"What has happened?" cried Laralynn, as she slid from her gray mare.

"My Lady, she had a visitor. It was a man that I had never seen before," replied Astra. "I saw them talking and called her back to the cottage because I felt danger surround him. When she tried to leave him, he grabbed her arm."

Astra's eyes filled with tears, and she collapsed to the ground. Laralynn knelt beside her and wrapped her arm around her shoulder.

"Baxter, try to get Aslev down from the roof," urged Laralynn as she wiped the tears from Astra's face.

"I thought her magic was taken from her," sniffled Astra. "I thought it was gone."

"What do you mean?"

"I saw purple sparks shoot from her fingertips, and I heard the man scream in pain before he rode away. It was then I noticed Aslev on the roof of the cottage."

"You're saying she did that using magic?"

"I don't think she purposely projected her magic. She seemed to react to his touch. Why did this happen? I thought her magic was gone."

Laralynn looked up to see Aslev wrapped in Baxter's arms, and her face buried in his chest. Happy to see her safely on the ground, she helped Astra stand.

"How long ago did this happen?" asked Laralynn.

"Just moments before you arrived," Astra replied, as she reached for her sister's hands and examined her fingers.

"If it's who I think it is, we need to go. He can't be that far ahead of us," said Laralynn. "Will you be all right, if we go?"

"Yes, we'll be fine."

Baxter followed Laralynn through the gate. Walking toward their horses, he could see the hoof prints in the dirt.

"He should be easy to follow," he said, as he pointed to the ground. "He left us a trail to follow."

"Then let's find him."

They raced along the road, and before long, they could see a single rider ahead of them.

Sure of who had frightened Aslev, Laralynn shouted, "Jario, your masquerade is up!"

Hearing his name, he turned to see what he dreaded most, Evergreen colors. Not wanting to be on the open road, he turned his stallion toward the cover of the forest and hoped he could out run them. He knew it would be two more days before the *Withering Rose* sailed from Woods Bay, and he would never avoid capture trying to hide in the village. He had to hide out in the mountains until it was safe to sail from the island. With his mind made up, he raced for Wintergreen Mountain.

Chapter 10

Ice

Jario had fooled no one by leaving his horse tethered near the cliffs of Wispet Canyon. On foot, there were only a few places he could hide. The Wispet Queen would never allow him to hide in the canyon, and if he made his way to Crimson Claw Castle, he would be greeted by a vampire ready to take his head. That left the Wintergreen Mountains as his only refuge.

They had spent all day following the footprints Jario had carelessly left in the snow as he wove aimlessly through the trees, but it was their abrupt end that had them more than a little confused. It appeared as if he had vanished mid-step into thin air. There was nothing ahead of them but a frozen lake surrounded by trees laden heavy with snow. It was obvious he had not obtained the *gift of flashing*, for he would have used it as soon as he knew that he was being followed. Clearly, the use of some other gift had assisted him, but what could have made his footprints vanish?

"We've lost him," grumbled Baxter. "He's outsmarted us."

"Where could he have gone?" asked Laralynn. "He wouldn't dare try to cross the lake, it's too dangerous. One wrong move and he could fall through the ice."

"I say good riddance to the traitor if he does, but I doubt Jario is that stupid." Baxter walked along the edge of the lake looking for any other footprints. "There has to be another trail. Look over there along the edge. He had to have gone around the lake."

Discouraged after finding nothing, Laralynn headed back toward Baxter. Out of the corner of her eye, she noticed a white rabbit scampering across the ice. Its sudden change in direction and frantic race for the trees caused her to search for any impending danger. Scanning the edge of the forest, she found nothing unusual. Drawing her attention back toward the spot where the rabbit had made his retreat, her eyes caught sight of a white wisp of something that looked like fog hovering over the ice.

"Baxter, do you see that?" she asked, as she pointed toward the center of the lake.

"See what?" He looked where she was pointing but saw nothing.

"That hazy cloud in the middle of the lake. It's like a fog has settled on the lake. I think something near it startled that rabbit."

"I still don't see anything."

"It's right in the middle of the lake. Can you use your gift of wind to move it? Some animal must be near it or hiding behind it."

"I can blow air across the lake, but you'll have to tell me if I move it since I can't see it."

"I will."

"Stand back, I don't want to hurt you. I've only done this a few times."

Laralynn stepped back away from the edge of the lake. She watched Baxter squat down near its edge and cup his hands around his mouth. A gentle whistling sound had filled the air before she saw flakes of snow swirl up into a ball and push across the ice. Satisfied with its size, he stood and waved his clenched fist back and forth making the ball of wind skim back and forth across the ice.

"Move it toward the center of the lake. The fog is in the

center."

Baxter moved his fist toward the center, and the wind followed.

"Stop! Keep it there. You are right in front of it."

Laralynn watched the fog fight against the wind. As it did, she could see ripples in the fog and a strange shimmer. It was then that she realized it wasn't fog; it was Jario's haze.

"Baxter, you can stop. I know what it is. It's Jario trying to hide behind his haze. The freezing temperature is turning his haze into a fog."

He opened his fist, and the wind immediately stopped swirling, and the snow fell to the ice.

"Since I can see him, I'm going to flash out to the lake and then flash him back to Evergreen."

"Not without me you aren't. He has hands of stone."

"I'll be careful."

"I'm still going with you. I'm stronger than you are."

"Come with me then. We'll both take him to the Command Center at Evergreen. Ready?"

Baxter nodded as he took hold of Laralynn's hand.

"On three . . . one . . . two . . . three.

Jario felt his haze waver and then disappear just before he saw Baxter and Laralynn standing before him. He knew Baxter had gifts, but Laralynn was a human. Humans were never given gifts by the Wispet Queen.

"How did you . . . flash?" stuttered Jario. "You aren't a vampire. I would know it if you were immortal."

"There are a lot of things she can do, traitor. Prepare yourself for the Evergreen dungeon. You're coming with us."

Baxter grabbed Jario's wrist and pulled his arm away from his body. Laralynn followed his lead and grabbed his other wrist with both hands. Jario tried to yank his arm away from her but to no avail. As he did, he felt the cloth bundle he had slung over his shoulder slip down to the bend of his elbow. The bundle dangled awkwardly from his arm while he tried to free himself from Baxter's strong grip. He pulled and twisted his arm until he was finally able to jerk his arm free. As he did, the sword he had so cleverly stolen slipped from the cloth and the point of the blade pierced the ice before it fell flat against the frozen lake.

"Get the sword, Laralynn," yelled Baxter, as he grabbed Jario's other wrist.

She quickly retrieved the sword from the ice and reached for Baxter's arm to prepare to flash. A cracking sound made her hesitate for only a moment to look down at the ice. Several fissures were spreading out under her boots from the spot where the sword had pierced the ice. Taking another step toward Baxter only caused more to streak across the ice.

"Don't move, Laralynn," ordered Baxter as he struggled to hold both of Jario's wrists.

"Go, Baxter, take him. I'll meet you back at Evergreen. Go now before we all fall through the ice."

Trusting Laralynn would follow him, Baxter nodded and vanished with Jario in tow.

She started to flash, but a feeling of nausea held her back, and a sharp pain drew her hand to her forehead.

"Don't pass out now, I need to tell mother of Jario's capture," she pleaded.

"Mother, can you hear me?" she whispered, as she searched for her mother's mind. *"Can you hear me?"*

"Yes, I can hear you."

"We've caught Jario. Baxter is flashing him back to the Command Center."

"I am with Preston and your father. We will see that he is secured, but why aren't you with him?"

"The ice began to crack when I lifted the Singing Sword from the ice."

"You have the sword?"

"Yes, I sent Jario ahead of me, but the sword started making a strange humming noise. I felt dizzy and a bit too nauseous to flash."

"Laralynn, you need to flash back to Evergreen."

"I can't, mother. I'm just not strong enough."

"Laralynn, Baxter has arrived, and I'm sending him back to get you."

Laralynn's ears began to ring, and the trees around the lake seemed to be spinning. Afraid she would fall, she sat down and placed the sword across her lap. While she waited for Baxter's return, the humming of the sword and the cracking of the ice grew louder with every passing moment. Placing her hands over her ears and closing her eyes, she tried to block out the painful sounds.

It was the sound of something smashing against the ice that drew her attention. There before her were Baxter and Jario wrestling like children on the ice.

"Stop it you fools!" she screamed at them. "The ice is cracking more and more with every move you make. We will all surely fall through the ice if you don't stop it now."

Baxter rolled off Jario and took a crouched protective stance in front of Laralynn as Jario stood.

"Why did you bring him back? He should be in the dungeon."

"It wasn't my intention. He grabbed my wrist as I flashed."

"Give me the sword," demanded Jario.

Baxter only laughed at his demand, "Do you think we are fools? Stay where you are."

"I could have used my gift of stone, but I didn't. I had an opportunity, but I wanted to show you that I mean you no harm. I am only here to retrieve the sword for Mistress Violeta. If I fail, I will be given my final death. Give it to me, and I'll leave this island and never return."

"Why should we trust you," asked Baxter. "The list of your crimes against Lady Lara, Evergreen, and others is long and unthinkable. Do you think we've overlooked the fact you stole the sword from Black Thistle Castle? For that crime, you will have to face Lord Gautier."

"I know I have given you no reason to trust me, but I swear to you that I am speaking the truth."

"The truth hardly makes up for your crimes. We have orders to take you back to Evergreen, and I intend to follow my orders."

"I can't let you do that. I'm not willing to die when that sword will save me."

Jario lowered his shoulder and rushed at Baxter knocking him backward into Laralynn. As her head hit the ice a loud crack followed by a sequence of popping sounds made them still. A moment of silence briefly calmed their fears as they all looked for an escape.

"Laralynn, take my hand," begged Baxter. "We need to get off this ice."

Seeing the sword had slipped from Laralynn's lap and rested beyond her reach, Jario slid across the ice on his stomach toward his prize. He managed to secure the hilt of the sword in his right hand as he tried to stand, but his stiff fingers caused the sword to slip from his hand down between two chunks of ice. Determined to make one last attempt to retrieve the sword, he leaned into the freezing water but lost his balance and fell headfirst into its icy depths.

"No!" screamed Laralynn, as the ice began breaking into pieces around her.

She struggled to grasp Baxter's hand, but the ice beneath them gave way, and she watched Baxter slip below the water's surface. Holding onto a small wedge of ice was the only thing keeping her afloat as she frantically searched for him. Not seeing him surface, she let herself sink down into the water in hopes of finding him, but she could only see darkness. Afraid the icy water would claim her as well, Laralynn forced her way to the surface for a much-needed breath. Just as she gasped to fill her lungs with air, a large chunk of ice slammed into the back of her head causing her body to still from the sharpness of the pain. As the pain began to fade, the darkness surrounded her and claimed her as its own. Laralynn drifted further and further down through the water. Unable to hold her breath any longer, she willingly allowed the icy water to fill her lungs. Giving herself over to death's gentle bidding, she closed her eyes and let her love for Baxter fill her final thoughts.

The sound of shattering glass and the rush of warm air

against her face startled Laralynn from a dream of a faceless man searching for her magical sword. Finding herself awake and floating within what seemed like a night's sky full of stars eased her fearful mind.

Death has surely claimed me and taken me to the most beautiful place, she thought.

She could hear someone cry out and then shout her name. Looking about, she saw nothing but the darkness and twinkling lights.

"Who is there?"

A gentle breeze brushed her cheek, and her name lingered in the air.

"Make yourself known. Who calls my name?"

Chapter 11

Alabaster

"No!" shouted Baxter as he ran to Laralynn's crumpled body. Kneeling next to her, he saw a shard of ice had penetrated her chest. He gently brushed the snow from her face and noticed a slight flutter of her eyelashes. "Laralynn, I'm here with you," he sighed, with relief. "Don't give up. Please, don't leave me."

The crunching of snow beneath Jario's boots gave away his approach.

"Don't stand too near me, Jario," snarled Baxter.

"What can I do . . . to help Lady Laralynn?" stammered Jario.

"Haven't you done enough? Look at her. If you hadn't stolen that sword, none of this would have happened."

"If you hadn't chased me, none of this would have happened. I would have left the island and all of you behind."

"You blame us for this? You are still the same arrogant bastard that refuses to take the blame for anything. If Laralynn dies, I promise to give you a death befitting a traitor."

Baxter drew Laralynn's cold hand up and pressed a kiss to her palm.

"Again, what can I do to help?" asked Jario.

Before Baxter could reply, they were swarmed by guards wearing tunics of white fur and carrying staffs bearing globes of pulsing turquoise light.

"Halt! You are under arrest," roared one of the guards. "You have trespassed the boundaries of our kingdom."

Jario turned to run but soon realized he was surrounded.

"Can't you see we need help?" blurted Baxter. "She is injured, and I fear that she will die without a healer."

"We will take your woman with you to the dungeon and see that she is treated by our healer."

"She is not my woman," snarled Baxter through gritted teeth. "She is Lady Laralynn of Evergreen Castle and should be treated thus. I will not stand for her to be hauled away to your dark dungeon."

"It will be up to Queen Nora to decide where she will be imprisoned. Stand and be bound. We will call for the Healer's Carriage to carry the Lady Laralynn to our Healing Room."

Baxter continued to hold Laralynn's hand in his own and tried to flash, but he couldn't feel his gifts. Wherever they were, their gifts were useless, and without them, they had no way to protect themselves.

"What is this place?" asked Baxter as he stood and moved his hands behind his back.

"This place is Alabaster, and it is ruled by King Teppo and Queen Nora," replied the guard. "You have entered the Pride's Realm of Silver Lions."

"You are lion shifters?" asked Jario.

"Yes, we are lion shifters, vampire. Does that surprise you?"

The guard standing next to him grabbed Jario's sword away from him.

"Be careful with that sword. I am charged with taking it to Mistress Violeta."

Ignoring Jario, another guard yanked his hands behind his back and bound glowing strips of turquoise leather around his wrists. Jario grabbed the guard's finger and tried to pull his gift of stone. Baxter noticed a look of confusion on Jario's face and knew he must have tried using his gift against the guard. With their weapons stripped from them and their wrists bound, they were completely at the mercy of their captors.

A carriage resembling a silver cage drawn by a lion appeared out of nowhere and hovered beside Laralynn. Two women dressed in flowing white gowns stepped from the carriage and knelt by her side.

"She is lingering in the darkness at the door of the Otherworld," whispered one of the women.

"I feel her searching for someone," replied the other woman. "She refuses to leave us, and her desire to stay is strong."

"Please help her," begged Baxter. "Please find a way to help Lady Laralynn."

Without saying another word, the women waved their hands in circles over Laralynn. As they stood and walked back to the carriage, Laralynn's body lifted from the ground and floated into the carriage. The women climbed in after her, and the carriage vanished.

Struggling to free himself from his bindings, Baxter snarled, "Where have you taken her?"

"She has been taken to the Queen's Healing Room. Now, let's get moving," barked the guard. "King Teppo will be waiting."

The guard, Baxter assumed to be the leader, led them toward an area full of cone-shaped columns rising from the wet ground. Baxter could hear water dripping from above and looked up to find nothing but darkness.

"What are those things?" he asked, being careful not to touch them.

"We call them Sentries," the guard replied. "They are what signaled your arrival through the portal."

"Portal? I don't understand how we came to be in Alabaster. We fell through the ice, nothing more. You must believe me, it was not our intention to come here."

"You can explain yourselves to King Teppo. He will decide your fate. For now, mind your footing. We have a treacherous path ahead of us."

Baxter nodded but kept his eyes examining everything

around him. He realized that without their gifts their only chance for escape would be to remember their path back to the sentries and find the hidden portal back to Wintergreen Mountain.

* * *

Upon entering the Queen's Healing Room, the women placed Laralynn on a long narrow table made from ice. Topaz, known to be the wisest of the healers, went about lighting the crystal orbs that were scattered about the room. Ruby, her sister, set to work by filling a basin with water filled with herbs. While letting the herbs steep, they carefully removed Laralynn's boots and clothing. With the aroma of lavender and mint filling the air, they cleaned the blood from around the ice shard that still protruded from her chest. After covering her with a linen cloth, Topaz and Ruby stood silently waiting for the arrival of their queen.

It wasn't long before Queen Nora entered the Healing Room. She was a tall, graceful woman with pale skin and gray-streaked white hair that hung in a long, intricate braid against her back. She was known for the kindness she showed to her people and her fierce protection of Teppo, the king, and her son, Satu. But, if you were brave enough to cross her, you would find a swift reaction to your betrayal. Many had thought her weak and tried to dethrone the king. They had all paid the ultimate price.

Nora made her way to Laralynn's side and placed her hand upon her forehead. Quickly removing it, she turned to face the healers.

"She is human. How did she pass through the portal?"

"We believe she fell through the ice that lies above Alabaster," replied Ruby.

"Why haven't you removed the shard from her chest?"

"My Queen, if we do, she will die. The shard has pierced her heart," replied Topaz.

87

"Is there no way to save her?"

"My Queen, her spirit is hovering at the door to the Otherworld. It is lost and has been searching for someone. We believe this someone could bring her spirit back to her body," explained Ruby. "We must keep the shard frozen until it returns. Sadly, when it does and the shard is removed, her life will end quickly."

"What do you know of her?"

"We heard her protector call her Lady Laralynn, and we found it odd that she has been gifted with magic," replied Topaz.

"A human with magic, this is rare."

"Also, she wore clothing befitting a man," offered Ruby. "We removed them and found a small dagger in her boot. Her tunic bore an emblem that we have never seen."

"Let me see it."

Ruby picked up the tunic and handed it to her queen. Nora unfolded the fabric to find a small emblem embroidered in gold threads. She ran her fingers over the standing lion holding a dagger.

"I know this marking. I have seen it before."

Nora searched her mind for where she had seen the standing lion. She remembered being taken by her mother and father to a place far from the ice and snow of Alabaster. The scent of pine was a memory she had long forgotten.

"As a child, I visited a castle that overlooked a sea of dark blue water. The banners that hung upon the stone walls held this emblem. While my parents discussed important matters, I played within the castle walls with two girls much younger than myself. Their names were Lara and Magna. I'm surprised that I remember their names. It was so long ago."

"Could she have come from this castle?" asked Topaz.

"I believe she could have come from that castle, and I believe there is more to this than a young woman falling through a portal. Take care to protect her. I must speak with Teppo."

"As you wish, My Queen," replied the women.

* * *

As Nora entered the Pride Hall, she saw Teppo and Satu were already seated. To the King's right stood his brother, Crew. To the King's left stood Commander Vitas with a scowl upon his face.

"My love, we have waited for you to begin the examination of our intruders. Have you learned anything from the young woman?" asked Teppo.

"Sadly, she is near death and could not speak. To my surprise, she is human," replied Nora.

"Human?" gasped Teppo as he glared at his commander. "How was she able to pass through the portal?"

Vitas pursed his lips and offered a reply of silence.

"My healers tell me she is gifted with magic," answered Nora as she took her seat next to Teppo.

The metal hinges of a wooden door groaned as it opened. Two lions entered the hall followed by Baxter, Jario, and two guards. They were led to the front and center of the hall and made to kneel before the king. Teppo stood and made his way down the stone steps to stand before them. With his hands behind his back, he began pacing back and forth in front of them as he put his thoughts in order.

"I am King Teppo," he boldly stated. "You have carelessly entered Alabaster. I want to know who you are and why you have done so."

Jario looked at Baxter and silently nodded toward the king hoping he would make an excuse for them both.

Baxter cleared his throat and straightened his shoulders. "My Lord, I am Lt. Baxter Marsh of the Evergreen Army. Myself and the Lady Laralynn were ordered to arrest Jario." He looked over at Jario's panicked expression and back at the king. "He was involved in the plot to kidnap the Lady Lara of Evergreen. He attacked Lady Kayleigh of Black Thistle and turned her guardian to stone. Recently, he stole a sword from Lord Gautier. He has been branded a thief and a traitor."

The king raised a brow and shook his head as he spoke, "These are serious crimes." Troubled by the charges, he turned to face Nora and smiled. "If someone attacked my queen, it would surely mean their death." He stood for a moment admiring his queen and then turned back to face Jario. With a furrowed brow, he waited for Jario to look up. "You have heard the Lieutenant. By the look upon your face, you are concerned for your life. What do you have to say in reply to these accusations?"

Jario closed his eyes and tried to think of something to say. He knew the charges were all true.

"I will be truthful, My Lord," he said, with his head bowed. "I did exchange a favor for the Lady Lara, but it was done for love. I had loved her long before Thomas caught her eye. I found restraint over my actions had abandoned me."

"I understand. Love makes us do foolish things. What of the Lady Kayleigh and her guardian?"

"I was forced by a witch to retrieve the tail of her wolf. Her guardian came to her aid and tried to kill me. I was only trying to protect myself."

"Finally, you are charged with stealing a sword from Lord Gautier."

"The Mistress Violeta ordered me to retrieve the sword. I must comply within nine moons, or I will be given my final death. You see, I had no choice."

Teppo stroked the gray stubble on his chin and pondered for a moment the words he had heard from Jario. Coming to a decision, he ordered Jario to stand.

"I have heard you repeat your crimes, make excuses for your actions, but never offer a single regret or apology. You have shown me no remorse for your actions."

Jario started to speak, but Teppo quickly raised his hand to demand silence.

"Jario, I order you to be imprisoned in the dungeon for your crimes until you can be returned to Evergreen Castle. I offer you this warning. Do not return to Alabaster, for I will personally see to your final death if you do."

Teppo returned to his throne. Without turning to look at Jario, he called to his lion guards. "Banyon, Sordin, escort the traitor to the dungeon."

Jario struggled against the lions, but he finally accepted his defeat once Banyon threatened him with an intimidating view of his teeth. He looked over his shoulder at Baxter for help but lost sight of him as the door was closed behind him.

"My Lord, what of the Lady Laralynn? Has she been healed?" asked Baxter. "May I see her?"

"Vitas, remove his bindings," ordered Teppo. "This lieutenant is no threat to us or Alabaster."

"My King, we still do not know how he came through the portal or if others wait to attack us," warned Vitas. "The woman is human. If she can pass through the portal others could follow. It puts us in great danger."

"I find him honorable, Vitas. There is no need for the bindings."

"As you wish, My King," Vitas responded and reluctantly descended the steps toward Baxter.

He cut the bindings from Baxter's wrists, but he quickly took a stance between his king and Baxter.

"The Lady Laralynn is near death," sighed Nora. "My healers have discovered the shard has pierced her heart. Once it is removed, she will die."

"Please take me to her," begged Baxter. "I know a way to save her."

Chapter 12

The Risk

Baxter walked in silence next to Queen Nora through the narrow hallway toward Laralynn. As they made one last turn, he could see the flickering candlelight coming from an open doorway. He listened carefully, but he couldn't hear her breathing. Her scent of fresh apples that he dearly loved was nowhere to be found. It was as though she no longer existed. Fearing that she was gone from him forever, he ran the remaining distance to see for himself.

Standing at the entrance to the small chamber, he could see Laralynn lying before him on a table of ice. A linen cloth covered her body up to the frozen shard that stood like a dagger claiming her heart. Her lips were blue, her skin was almost translucent, and her bright copper hair had faded. This was not his Laralynn, and he was sure she had left him.

Baxter could feel Queen Nora standing behind him, but he hadn't noticed the woman standing near Laralynn until she stepped forward from the shadows. Her outstretched arm and open palm invited him to come forward.

"Do not worry. She has not left us," the woman whispered. "Come stand by her side. I believe she is searching for you."

"What do you mean?" he asked, as he slowly walked toward Laralynn.

"She is hovering at the door to the Otherworld. She has been searching for someone, and we believe this someone could bring her spirit back to her body."

Baxter lifted the edge of the linen cloth and reached for her hand. Kneeling on one knee, he closed his eyes and kissed the back of her hand.

"I'm here, Laralynn, and I will never leave you. I'm waiting for you to come back to me. My love, you must try to come back to me."

He could feel the gentle touch of a hand upon his shoulder and looked up to see Queen Nora's sympathetic smile. As he stood, he kept Laralynn's hand clasped within his own.

"You must know that even if she comes back, she will die when the shard is removed," sighed Nora. "Sadly, it has penetrated her heart. There is no way for us to save her. It would be best to send her to the Otherworld with your love and your blessing."

"I won't let her go to the Otherworld alone. If she must go, then I will go with her, for we were meant to be together. If fate demands it, we shall be together in the Otherworld for all eternity." He bowed his head and drew Laralynn's hand to his lips before tucking it back under the linen cloth. "I will never leave her."

"Earlier, you spoke of saving her. Have you decided it cannot be done?"

"I believe that I can coax her back, but I would need my gifts returned to me. They vanished the moment I fell through the portal."

"The Sentries are charged with removing them for our protection."

"How do I get them back? Without them, I can't speak to her mind, and she can't speak to mine."

"I can return them, My Queen," offered Topaz.

At first, Baxter was overjoyed. Then, his thoughts immediately went to Jario. He realized, if Jario's gifts were returned, revenge would be foremost on his mind. He would never forgive them for sending him back to the dungeon.

"Will it put Alabaster in danger?" asked Nora.

"It will cause the Sentries to sleep, leaving the portal unguarded."

Baxter's concern caused him to ask, "Does this mean Jario will also retain his gifts?"

"Yes, his gifts will be returned," replied Topaz.

"I hear a sense of dread in your voice, Baxter. Do I dare put my people in danger to help one young woman?" asked Nora.

"There is no doubt that Jario is dangerous. He has a number of gifts that could harm your people. It is best I explain them so that you understand the risk that is before you."

"I will listen, but if the risk is too great, my answer will be no. I must protect my people."

Baxter nodded and carefully explained, "He has the gift of haze which allows him to vanish before your eyes. With his gift of compulsion, he could demand anything of you, and you would comply without question. Due to a spell cast by a warlock, he can change his appearance to any masculine human form. The most dangerous of his gifts is the gift of stone which allows him the ability to turn someone to stone by a single touch."

"They sound more like weapons than gifts. I now understand the sense of dread I heard in your voice," she replied.

"If care is taken to isolate him, the risk should be lessened.

"But still a risk to everyone at Alabaster."

"Yes, he would still prove to be a risk; however, he does have weaknesses. If he walks in daylight, his flesh will burn until there is nothing left of him but ash.

"Unfortunately, daylight will not assist our defenses since the sun is rarely present over Alabaster."

"He must consume blood. If he doesn't feed, the hunger that rages in all vampires will cause the madness to destroy him. Eventually, he will succumb to a final death."

"Baxter, I will not starve him to death to protect my people."

"Then return my gifts so that I can take Jario from Alabaster back to Evergreen. I am sure he will be eager to leave and put up little resistance. With him gone, he can no longer be a danger to your people. I only ask that you allow me to return to help Laralynn."

"After hearing of Jario's many crimes and his gifts, I find it was wise for the Sentries to protect us. I must speak to Teppo about your need to have your gifts returned, and your offer to remove Jario. Once we have made a decision, I will return to give you our answer. Until then, you may stay by Laralynn's side."

"I hope your answer comes soon."

Nora nodded and turned to leave. When she reached the doorway, she froze in place for a moment and then slowly turned to face Baxter.

"You said that Jario must consume blood or face what you call the madness."

"Yes, this is true."

"Will the same thing happen to you?"

"It will, but you must trust me when I say that I don't drink human blood. Your people are in no danger from me. Lady Lara forbade the drinking of human blood long ago. We are only allowed to drink the blood from animals."

Nora raised a brow and tilted her head.

"I'm not sure that makes me feel much better. You forget we are a community of lions."

Baxter offered a forced smile. He had forgotten.

"Our woodsmen are kept busy hunting in the forests that surround our castle, and I'm sure we can satisfy your need for animal blood. I must warn you; do not give me a reason to worry."

He understood why Queen Nora was concerned and knelt on one knee, drew his fist across his chest, and bowed his head.

"I swear to you that while I am here in Alabaster, I will honor your commands and protect you as my queen with my life."

Overwhelmed by his pledge, Nora placed her hand upon his

head.

"I accept your pledge of honor and protection. While you are here in Alabaster, you will be known as the Queen's Sentinel. If we are to allow our Sentries to sleep, we will need someone to keep watch over Alabaster and its portal."

"You honor me, My Queen."

Nora looked over at Laralynn and then down at Baxter's bowed head. She knew he would be loyal to her and all of Alabaster. His devotion to Laralynn had proven it. Without saying a word, she quietly left to search for Teppo.

* * *

After finding only Vitas and Crew in the Council Chamber, they advised her the king had retired to his bedchamber. Nora was surprised, for Teppo never retired during the waking hours. He would have thought it rude with visitors within Alabaster's walls.

As Nora opened the door to their bedchamber, she called out to Teppo but heard no reply. The hearth held a small smoldering fire that had not been fed since the morning, and his favorite chair was empty. Sure that Vitas had misunderstood his king, she turned to continue her search. It was then that she heard the sound of muffled snoring and noticed the heavy drapes that surrounded their bed were drawn.

Pulling the drape back, she could see Teppo on his back with his hands resting on his stomach. If it weren't for the rhythmic serenade he was offering her, she would have thought him ill. Gently, she placed her hand upon his. He stirred for a moment and then continued his snoring.

"Teppo, my love, you must wake up." She waited a moment and tried again. "Teppo, I need you to wake up."

He snorted and mumbled something about bitter wine and snapped his tongue on the roof of his mouth.

"Teppo, can you hear me?"

With his eyes still closed he replied, "I hear you, Nora. Could you not see that I was sleeping?"

"I could see it and hear it too, my love. You are a melodious king."

He opened his eyes and rolled over on his side to look at her.

"You have my attention. What couldn't wait until my nap was complete? Have more vampires fallen through the portal?"

"No, the portal is closed," she said, as she crawled up onto the bed and let the drape close behind her. "However, I must speak to you about the portal and the Sentries."

Teppo pushed himself up and stuffed a large pillow behind his back. Taking her hands in his, he nodded for her to continue.

"I have taken the lieutenant to see the woman that fell through the portal with him. Sadly, a shard of ice pierced her heart. Her spirit was separated from her body, and she is searching for someone to save her."

"Have Topaz and Ruby been unable to heal the woman?"

"They cannot remove the shard until her spirit has rejoined her body."

"It is unfortunate, but this was not our doing. What does this have to do with the portal and the Sentries?"

"I wish to have Topaz make the Sentries sleep."

"What?" he growled. "You would have us left unprotected? Have you lost your mind, woman?"

Teppo let go of her hands and threw his legs over the side of the bed with a huff. Flinging back the drape, he stormed from the bed. Nora crawled across the bed after him.

"I beg you to listen to me, Teppo." She stood with her hands grasping his arms and her face against his back. She could feel the rapid beat of his heart, and she knew she had angered him. "Please listen to what I have to say. I know you want to protect Alabaster. I truly believe it would protect Alabaster."

"How could this possibly protect Alabaster?"

Teppo turned and glared down at Nora as he waited for her answer.

"It would allow Baxter to take Jario from the dungeon back

to Evergreen. We would be free of the traitor and the threat of his dangerous gifts."

Teppo began to pace back and forth in front of her. The sound of his heavy breathing and the gnashing of teeth worried her. She had not seen him this upset since Satu had become lost in the *Floating Forest* after running away.

"My love, Baxter has made a pledge to honor our commands and protect us. He did so willingly. It was nothing I asked of him."

"Words are easily spoken, my dear Nora. He is not from Alabaster. He owes no allegiance to us. I will not allow it."

Nora sank to the floor and covered her face with her hands to shield the tears she knew were coming.

"Don't cry, my love. You know it breaks my heart when you do."

Feeling remorseful for the anger he had shown Nora, Teppo knelt to comfort her. Gently pulling her hands away from her face, he leaned in and kissed her tears away.

"I cannot bear to see you sad. Take me to see Baxter, and I will listen to his plan." He could see her smile as he brushed a tear from her cheek. "I promise you nothing, but I will listen."

As Teppo stood, he lifted Nora to her feet and wrapped his arms around her. He could feel his tunic dampen from the last of her tears, and it saddened him. After kissing the top of her head, he took a step back and lifted her chin to grant him access to her mouth. He leaned in and softly brushed his lips against hers. Hearing her sigh pleased him.

"You are my undoing," he whispered. "I will never get enough of you."

Reaching for her hand, he stumbled and thought he had lost his footing on the hem of her gown. Looking down at his boots, a sudden burst of light made him close his eyes for relief. He grabbed for Nora's arm to steady his footing but felt himself begin to fall.

"Teppo, what's wrong?" cried Nora as she watched him slump to the floor.

Cradling his head in her lap, she screamed for the guards for help. They burst into the bedchamber and knelt to assist their king. Looking up, she saw Vitas standing in the doorway. She was sure she had seen him smile before he ran to her side.

Chapter 13

Betrayal

Nora hurried behind the guards led by Vitas as they carried their king to the Healing Room. While entering the chamber, she saw Baxter standing next to someone else covered in white linen.

"Who else has fallen ill?" asked Nora as she placed her hand upon Teppo's chest in search of a heartbeat.

"It is Satu, My Queen," replied Ruby. "Topaz and I were about to send word of his arrival."

"My son is ill? When did this happen?"

"He fell ill within his chamber, and his servant carried him to us not long after you left to find the king."

"It must be some strange illness brought here by the intruders," snarled Vitas while pointing toward Baxter. "He and the traitor were near Satu and even nearer to our king. There is no other explanation."

"Yet, I still stand after being in their presence more than the king or my son," snapped Nora.

She noticed the guards back away from their king toward the hallway. Seeing the fear in their eyes, she shook her head in dismay. Her intuition was correct, Vitas had chosen guards that would be faithful to him rather than the king.

"I see the guards back away like cowards. Did they not offer a pledge to protect the king and Alabaster with their lives?"

A single guard stepped forward and bowed his head. "Forgive me, My Queen. I am ashamed that I have wronged you."

"I see there is still one honorable guard left within Alabaster." Turning to Vitas, she continued her verbal assault, "I expect you to discipline these men that have broken their pledge and teach them what it means to be honorable. Now, leave us."

"My Queen, you could still be in danger. As the King's Regent, I implore you to leave this chamber for your own protection." Expecting her to comply, Vitas reached for her arm. "Let me escort you back to your chamber."

"I will not leave Teppo or my son, understood? As you can see, a guard stands ready to protect me, and what better place to be than the Healing Room with Topaz and Ruby if I should fall ill."

Vitas flinched at her firm rejection of his request but nodded a show of understanding. "Yes, My Queen," replied Vitas through clenched teeth. He bowed his head and quickly left the chamber with his disgraced guards on his heels.

"Barkus, you may stand guard outside in the hallway. I expect no visitors, and if there should be someone brave enough to bother me, I expect you to turn them away, understood?"

"Yes, My Queen," he replied.

"Now, what have you discovered? Topaz, what is wrong with my son?" Nora asked.

"We found no signs of fever, rash, or sweating; however, we did find a slight discoloration of his tongue."

"Poison," offered Baxter.

"We came to the same conclusion," sighed Ruby. "We have found the same to be true of the king."

"Before Teppo fell ill in our bedchamber, he was sleeping. I found it odd that he would be sleeping during the waking hours with visitors in Alabaster. As I tried to wake him, he mumbled something about bitter wine."

"It would be easy enough to pour poison into a goblet of wine," reasoned Baxter. "A slight of hand, a back turned to the king to shield someone's actions, or even a pitcher tainted with poison brought from the kitchen would be without suspicion."

"Who would do such a thing?" gasped Nora. "Our people love their king."

"I doubt this was an act by only one person. It could be a plot by several to overthrow the king and lay claim to the throne. If I were to blame someone, I would blame Vitas. I have seen that same resentment in Jario's eyes. I saw the way he glared at you when you stood up to him. He is hungry for the king's power."

"I have never liked Vitas, but he has never been unfaithful to Teppo or to me."

"We will know soon enough. To blame Jario or me for an illness would be difficult without proof. If Vitas knows poison was used, he will bring the proof and his guards to arrest me. It is just a matter of time."

"I just can't believe he would do this. Even if the king and my son die, Crew would be put on the throne, not Vitas."

"You heard what Vitas said. He is the King's Regent."

"The king's brother is weak. He has always relied on Teppo for everything. Without his direction, he would look to Vitas."

"There you have it. Vitas has the most to gain from their deaths."

"I will need proof, as well. My people will demand it."

"I believe that you know I did not poison the king or your son. I swear to you that I had nothing to do with this treasonous act."

"I know in my heart that you tell the truth, but it will not be enough for my people. Superstition and fear will sway those that are unsure to believe Vitas' accusations."

"Then, let me ask again for one kindness. Let me have a few moments to reach out to Laralynn and bring her spirit back to her body. If I can bring her back, my only hope to save her is to turn her. If I don't, she will die. I know she would want me to do this for her."

"Let me think on it. I told Teppo of your desire, and it made him quite unhappy to hear of it. I will have to answer for my actions if anything should happen that puts Alabaster in danger."

"I am at your mercy, My Queen. I will wait for your decision and accept what you decide. It is yours to make."

Nora knew that everything Baxter had told her was true, but she had to have proof. She could not arrest Vitas without it.

Oh, Teppo, I need your strength to find the person that did this to you and our son.

* * *

Nora had stayed by the bedsides of Teppo and Satu for two days and two nights. There had been no change in their condition, and she feared they might never wake from their deep sleep. She continued to fight her own desire to sleep until Topaz insisted she should rest. With great reluctance, she allowed Barkus to escort her to her bedchamber. Once there, she bolted her door and prepared for bed.

Longing for Teppo, she clutched his pillow tightly against her body. Inhaling his scent from its linen covering, she closed her eyes and waited for sleep to claim her. Instead, her mind wandered back to the sight of Vitas at her doorway and the pleasure he seemed to take in seeing Teppo's head in her lap. She did not realize it at the time, but he rarely came to the king's bedchamber door on his own. A guard would have been sent if Teppo was needed.

He wanted to see Teppo and make sure the poison had done its job, she thought. He must be behind this, but how can I prove it?

Nora threw back the coverlet and swung her legs over the side of the bed. Without hesitation, she slid off the bed while lifting her sleeping gown over her head and throwing it to the floor. After dressing as quickly as she could, she headed for the door.

To her surprise, the hallway outside her door was empty. Vitas had left her unguarded. She thought that odd since both the king and his son had fallen ill.

Has he no concern for his queen's well-being?

Creeping as quietly as she could through the hallways, she made her way toward Crew's door. She could see the door was open by the firelight that reflected on the stone floor. Moving closer, she could hear voices arguing.

"You will do as I say. If not, I will prove that you poisoned your brother and your nephew. You will die a traitor's death, and I will enjoy watching it."

It was Vitas' voice; she was sure of it. Before she could take another step, Nora heard a loud smack and then a woeful moan that sent shivers down her spine. Unsure of what to do, she risked taking one more step. Standing dangerously close to the open door, she listened to every word that Vitas said. He recounted everything he had done and how he would blame the intruders for poisoning the king. Another loud smack let Nora know that Vitas had slapped Crew across the face again.

"You will be nothing but a puppet king. Do you know what that means? You will take your direction from me. I will control the strings. Do you understand? You will do nothing without my approval," snarled Vitas.

"Yes, I understand," mumbled Crew.

"You will lead the guards to arrest Baxter and send him and the Lady Laralynn to the dungeon. There, they will stay until they rot. Now, get yourself cleaned up. You are the king. It is time to start acting like it."

Nora hurried as quietly as she could back to her bedchamber door. As she touched the handle, she thought of Baxter and Laralynn. She knew what she had to do. Lifting the hem of her skirt, she turned and ran as fast as she could.

* * *

"I heard him, Baxter," Nora gasped, trying to catch her

breath. "I heard him admit knowledge of the poison. He is, as you said, hungry for the king's power."

"How did you learn of this?" asked Baxter.

"I stood outside Crew's door hidden in the shadows like a thief." As she ran her hand over Teppo's leg, she looked back at Baxter. "He plans to arrest you and take you both to the dungeon."

"If he does, it will surely be the end of us," replied Baxter. "Unless you are willing to let the Sentries sleep long enough for me to flash Laralynn back to Evergreen."

"If Vitas and Crew come with the guards to arrest you and find you gone, they will know I have discovered their plot. I will find myself in the dungeon alongside Jario with no hope of ever escaping."

"Sadly, there is truth in your words, and I can't allow harm to come to you. After all, it was not your fault that we found ourselves in Alabaster."

"There might be another way."

"You have a plan?"

"We know the guards will come for you. Once you are in the dungeon, you will be forgotten, left there to die."

"Can you devise a plan that does not include us dying?"

"Hear me out, Baxter," she smiled. "I think what I have in mind will work."

Baxter nodded and waited to hear the plan that would either offer them a way out of Alabaster or bring a guaranteed final death.

"Vitas' guards will take you to the dungeon. Once they have left you alone in your cells, I will ask Topaz to allow the Sentries to sleep. It will be up to you to silence the guards and compel them to take the blame for your escape. In return for allowing the Sentries to sleep, I have one condition."

"What is your condition?"

"You must promise me that you will not return to Evergreen until Teppo and Satu have been healed. If you cannot promise this, I will not allow the Sentries to sleep."

"Is there a place where we can hide and find the food that we require?"

"I can take you to the *Floating Forest*. There is a stone cottage hidden among the trees that could offer you safety. It was where I found Satu when he ran away. No one else knows of it."

"For a chance to save Laralynn, I accept your condition."

"Topaz, Laralynn must be dressed before the guards arrive. We'll need to cut a hole in a tunic to fit around that shard and let's do this quickly. We haven't much time."

Chapter 14

The Plan

Jario stood from his mound of rancid straw and grabbed the bars of his cell as he watched Baxter thrown into the cell next to him. To his surprise, the light from a single blazing torch offered him a glimpse of the Lady Laralynn carried awkwardly between two guards. The shard of ice reflected the flames and still stood as a reminder of her fall. It was the reckless way the guards dropped her on a thin layer of straw that caused him to cry out in her defense.

"Take care with the Lady Laralynn!" blurted Jario.

"Shut your mouth, or I'll do it for you," shouted the dungeon guard.

The cell doors slammed, and a ring full of keys clanged against each other as each cell door was locked.

"Enjoy your new friends," laughed the guard before he closed the heavy wooden door and threw the bolt, leaving them in silence.

The last time Jario had seen Baxter, he found himself standing before King Teppo as he confessed his crimes. As a result, he had been locked in the dungeon. Now, Baxter and Laralynn shared the dungeon darkness.

What crimes did they commit?

Jario heard Baxter groan and watched as he sat up holding

his head. He could smell blood and knew that Baxter had been wounded. His fangs descended, and he longed for a taste of it.

"Welcome to the pit of eternal suffering," smirked Jario. "I see that even you could not charm the king into allowing you to leave this place."

Crawling toward the cell next to him, he released a sigh of relief when he saw the shard had not been removed from Laralynn's chest.

"I see the king has shown no sign of mercy toward the Lady Laralynn or yourself. What crimes did you commit?" asked Jario.

Turning toward Jario, he moved close enough to see his face.

"We have committed no crimes," he replied. "We have merely been caught in a plot to remove the king from his throne. The king and his son have been poisoned, and we have all been blamed."

"So, we are doomed," Jario mumbled, as he turned and slumped against the bars in defeat.

"No, if all goes well, I may have a way to return us to Evergreen, but I will need your help."

"You want me to help you return me to the Evergreen dungeon? I'll be dead in nine moons if I don't return the sword to Mistress Violeta. I may as well stay here and save myself the humiliation."

Baxter looked over his shoulder at Laralynn's limp body and turned back to face Jario.

"What is your price, Jario? What is your price to help me?"

Jario chewed on his bottom lip as he pondered Baxter's question.

"I require safe passage to the Isle of Flames with the *Singing Sword*."

"If we get out of here, I give you my word that I will see you safely back to the Isle of Flames with the *Singing Sword*, but in return, you must give me your word that you will help me."

A spark of hope ignited Jario's interest as he pressed his face against the bars, "I give you my word that I will help you. Now, what is your plan?"

"Queen Nora has promised to help us. In return, we must help her."

"This sounds like an unending circle of everyone helping everyone. Do me a favor and explain the details. I don't want to do anything that would cause me to be left behind."

Baxter stepped closer to Jario to allow him to speak just above a whisper. The last thing he needed was for the guard to overhear his plan.

"Topaz, one of the healers, will cause the Sentries to sleep long enough to allow us to use our gifts. I will flash us outside of the cells. We must draw the guard inside and compel him to allow me to leave the dungeon."

"Wait, aren't we going with you?"

"I need you to keep watch over Laralynn while I meet Queen Nora at the top of the stone steps. She will lead me outside the castle walls."

"So, that gets you out of the castle. When do I get out?"

"It will be daylight and not safe for a vampire without the gift of walking in daylight."

What if the medallion has lost its magic, thought Jario. I won't survive without the gift in the sunlight.

"I don't have the gift, but Mistress Violeta placed a medallion within my chest to keep me safe from the sun's rays. I haven't been in the sun since falling through the portal and can't be sure the magic will still protect me."

"Unless you want to chance turning to ash, we should assume the magic was lost as you passed through the portal."

Jario nodded. He understood the risk he would be taking if he had to stand in daylight without protection, but he still worried about being left behind.

"I'll ask again. When do I get out?"

"There is more to the plan, Jario. I beg you to listen and not waste our precious time."

Jario angrily bit the inside of his mouth but nodded.

"The queen will shift into her lioness form and carry me to a place she calls the *Floating Forest*. She has told me of a stone cottage where we can safely hide and care for Laralynn. Once I have seen the path, I can flash her back to the castle and then return here, to the dungeon. From here, it will be easy to flash you and Laralynn to the cottage."

"What happens once we arrive at the cottage?"

"I will try to speak to Laralynn's mind and bring her back to her body. If she returns, I will remove the shard that has pierced her heart."

"If you remove that shard, she will die, Baxter."

"I am going to turn her. It is the only way to save her, and I will need your help to see her through it."

"I said I will help you, and I will."

"Good, there is more."

"More?"

"Once Laralynn is safe to be around others, we will return to the castle to help Queen Nora take back King Teppo's throne."

"How can we help Queen Nora?"

"Laralynn can heal Teppo and her son with her gift of healing. Once Teppo awakens, he can reclaim his throne, and we can leave Alabaster."

"When do we acquire the sword?"

"I plan to ask for those items that were taken from us. The sword was one of those items."

"You surprise me, Baxter. You have a well thought out plan. You learned much from the Evergreen Army and from me."

"Well, I won't be bragging until Laralynn has recovered, we are free of this place, and you have been taken to the Isle of Flames."

"What will Lady Lara do to you for allowing me to go free?"

"I'm not sure, but it will be worth it if Laralynn survives."

"You must truly love her?"

"I do, Jario, with every bit of my being. Without Laralynn, I would be lost."

A silence lingered between them until Jario asked, "What do we do now?"

"We wait for our gifts."

* * *

Baxter was awakened by a strange tapping noise. He looked over at Jario and found that he was sound asleep with his mouth wide open and his head tilted back against the stone wall. Looking toward Laralynn, he could see that she hadn't moved since the guards dropped her to the floor. He couldn't figure out where the noise was coming from. Fearing rats had invaded Laralynn's cell, he began crawling over to the bars to scare them away. As he neared the base of the bars, his hand came down in something wet.

What is this?

Smelling his hand, he found it to be water and wondered where it was coming from. It was then that panic consumed him. He stood and moved about the cell trying to see the reflection of the torch in the shard of ice. There wasn't enough light. He couldn't see it. Without thinking, he clenched his hands into fists, and they burst into flames. His biggest fear was realized when he saw that the ice shard was beginning to melt. Stepping back away from Laralynn, he looked down at his hands. Nora had done what she had promised. She allowed Topaz to make the Sentries sleep, and his gifts had been returned. Not waiting for Jario to wake, he extinguished the fire, flashed into Jario's cell, and offered him a swift kick to the sole of his boot. Jario's eyes flew open.

"Our gifts are back. It's time, but we need to hurry," whispered Baxter. "The ice shard is melting."

Baxter grabbed Jario by the arm, and the next thing Jario knew, he was standing on the outside of the cell.

"Do you remember our plan?" asked Baxter.

Jario nodded and then shouted for the guard. It seemed as though it took forever before they heard the bolt of the door begin to move. The guard pulled the door open and stepped forward carrying a burning torch.

"How did you get out?" barked the guard.

Jario grabbed his tunic and drew his eyes to his own.

"You will obey my every word. Hand the torch to the man beside you," ordered Jario. The guard handed the torch to Baxter. "You have decided to release the prisoners from their cell and allow Baxter to leave the dungeon. Once he is gone, you will return to your station and lock the door. If asked about the prisoners, you will tell them that all is quiet and secure."

Baxter walked through the open doorway followed by the guard. He heard the door close and the bolt slide back into place as he began to climb the stone steps. One by one he cautiously climbed toward who he hoped would be waiting for him. When he saw Queen Nora standing at the top of the steps, he knew the plan would work.

"I thought you would never get here," she whispered. "I waited for you, and finally had to descend those narrow steps to draw your attention."

"Was that you that made the tapping?"

"Yes, I sent the guard away and tapped on the door. It was the only thing I could think of to do."

"Well, I'm here now. Let's be on our way. I fear I am running out of time. The ice shard is melting."

Nora moved at a quick pace through the hallways with Baxter on her heels until she came to a large tapestry hanging on the wall. Pulling it back, she twisted the handle of a wooden door and pushed it open. Following her inside and closing the door, Baxter was confronted by another set of stone steps leading down.

"The steps are treacherous," she whispered. "Mind your footing, or we'll both end up in a heap, broken and battered. The door at the bottom of the steps opens to a tunnel that will take us beyond the wall that surrounds the castle."

"Let me go first. If you should stumble, I will be able to catch you," he replied.

Gathering her skirt and twisting it over her arm, Nora began to descend the steps behind Baxter. The narrow, steep steps slowed their pace, but they finally reached the tunnel entrance.

"Stand back, Baxter. I am going to shift. We will move much faster if I carry you through the tunnel."

It had taken only a moment before a large silver-gray lioness stood before him. Her paws were the size of a man's head, and she stood as tall as a pony. Feeling a bit intimidated, he stepped back even further. The lioness crouched before him and waited.

"Baxter, I won't hurt you. We must hurry," Nora's lioness spoke to him.

Her voice washed away his fear, and he hurried toward her. Climbing onto her back, he wrapped his arms around her neck. As she stood, he shifted his weight to secure his hold and nudged her with his boots to let her know he was ready. He felt a sudden jolt as she leaped into the dark tunnel, and then the cool air rushing against his face. She moved effortlessly through the tunnel as if she were flying.

It wasn't long before he could feel her pace begin to slow and the light begin to replace the tunnel's darkness. As she stepped from the tunnel, the sunlight and a burst of warmth surrounded them. The snow and ice were nowhere to be found. Before him, a meadow laid covered in yellow and white wildflowers amongst green sweet grass that gently swayed in the breeze. Looking up, he couldn't believe his eyes. She had called it the *Floating Forest*. He had thought it to be an island covered in trees in the middle of a lake. It was nothing as he had imagined. What floated in the sky, with no attachment to the earth beneath it, was an island surrounded by the clouds in the sky and covered with trees.

Nora knelt and allowed Baxter to slip to the ground. In an instant, she had returned to her human form.

"It's beautiful," Nora sighed. "It took my breath away the first time I saw it."

Baxter nodded but continued to stare up at the sky.

"Follow me; the portal to the mountain is near."

Without hesitation, she lifted her skirt and headed toward a small pond. Standing at the water's edge, he could see his reflection staring back at him.

"What now, My Queen?" he asked.

"Don't you see it?"

"See what?"

"Don't look down at the water. Look out over the water."

Baxter looked across the surface of the water and saw something shimmering just above its surface.

"Is that the portal?"

"Yes, it is the portal to the *Floating Forest*. Take my hand and walk with me through the portal."

Baxter took Nora's outstretched hand.

"Don't be nervous. I won't let you fall," she smiled.

Baxter matched her steps, one for one, as they walked across the surface of the water and through the shimmering portal to a forest thick with trees.

"The cottage is just beyond those trees."

"Those trees . . . which trees, there are trees everywhere."

"I told you the cottage was well hidden," she laughed. "Now, let's hurry."

Nora wove her way through the trees never letting go of Baxter's hand. He could hear her counting her steps as they walked.

"We are almost there. It is just beyond that hollow tree."

Baxter searched for the cottage, but his eyes failed him.

"I see nothing but trees, My Queen."

"Look again, Baxter. Focus on the hollow tree."

He stared at the tree, and suddenly, he could see the cottage.

"I see it. I see it clearly, now," he gasped. "Let's get inside, and I'll flash us back to Alabaster."

They made their way into the cottage. Baxter took in the cots, table, chairs, and hearth.

"It will do, My Queen. It will do just fine."

"There is nothing more I can do for you. Take us back to Alabaster."

Baxter took her hand in his, and in an instant, they stood at the top of the steps leading to the dungeon.

"It is all up to you, Baxter. I hope to see you soon."

"Thank you for this kindness. I will do all that I can."

Without another word, Baxter vanished back to the dungeon. He could see Jario sitting cross-legged in front of Laralynn's cell with his back against the bars. When he saw Baxter, he jumped up to greet him.

"The shard is almost gone. We need to hurry."

Baxter quickly flashed into Laralynn's cell. He knelt beside her and laid her arms across her stomach. Lifting her from the floor, he settled her head against his shoulder and flashed next to Jario.

"Hold onto my arm, and don't let go," ordered Baxter.

Jario complied, and they vanished.

Chapter 15

Her Turn

Baxter laid Laralynn on a cot covered with a well-worn cushion stuffed with feathers. It was nestled in the corner of the one room cottage and well protected from the light.

"Baxter, it won't be long before the shard is melted. Will you be able to reach her in time?" asked Jario.

"I will try, but I'm afraid she may have given up on me since she hasn't heard from me."

He noticed a small stool was tucked partway under the cot. Retrieving it, he sat down next to her. Taking Laralynn's hand, he lifted it to his lips and let his mind call to her.

"Laralynn, can you hear me? I need you to answer me. Laralynn, can you hear me?"

He waited but heard nothing but bitter silence.

"Laralynn, it's Baxter. I know you are there. The healers told me you were searching for someone. Are you searching for me? You need not search any longer. I'm right here. I'm holding your hand and waiting for you to come back to me."

Again, he was offered nothing but silence.

"Are you afraid, my love? You needn't be. Tell me where you are. I am trying to help you. Listen to my voice and let it guide you back."

As he started to call her name again, he heard a faint sigh.

"Is that you, Laralynn? Did I wake you? I'm sure you've grown tired of waiting to hear my voice, but I'm here, Laralynn. I'm here waiting for you."

"Who calls my name in the darkness?" she softly replied. "Are you friend or foe?"

"It's me, Baxter. Come closer, Laralynn, and follow the sound of my voice."

"Where are you? I cannot see you. The sky has wrapped its darkness around me and only offers the starlight to light my way."

"I am beside you holding your hand. I am waiting for you to open your eyes."

"I must keep my eyes closed."

"Why, are you afraid of something?"

"No, I'm not afraid. I don't want to see the woman that begs me to follow her. She is always there reaching her arms out to me."

"Laralynn, stay away from the woman. I want you to listen to my voice. Can you do that?"

"I will listen. Are you coming to be with me? I miss you. It is lonely here among the stars."

"I am lonely too, but I want you to come to me."

"I don't know how to leave this place."

"I'm going to help you, but first, I must tell you something. I don't want you to be frightened, but I want you to know what has happened."

"I am listening."

"When you fell through the ice and the portal, your spirit separated from your body. I believe this happened because you were injured. A shard of ice has pierced your heart, Laralynn."

"Am I going to die? Is that why I am here? Is that why the woman begs me to follow her? Is she here to take me to the Otherworld?"

"Your spirit must have thought you were going to die, but your body was too strong to give into death's call."

"You want me to rejoin my body, but if I do, I will die."

"I want you to rejoin your body, Laralynn. I need you to rejoin your body, for I have a plan to keep you with me."

"Will you help me like Oliver helped you? Will I be like you, Baxter?"

"Yes."

"I need you to help me come back. It is dark, and I can't find my way back to you."

"Do you remember how we traveled from Black Thistle to Evergreen?"

"Yes, we flashed back to Evergreen."

"Think of your body as the place you want to go. Flash back to your body, and I will be here waiting for you."

"Do you promise?"

"I promise I will be here waiting for you."

Baxter waited for a reply but none came. He searched Laralynn's face for any sign that she had returned, but she looked the same.

"She spoke to me, Jario. She's trying to come back."

"Can she do it on her own?"

"I hope she can. There is nothing I can do but call to her."

Time passed slowly, and he feared he would lose her. Not willing to give up, he continued to hold her hand and whisper words of love hoping she could still hear him. He was so focused on listening for her voice that he didn't notice the changes that were taking place.

"Look at her face, she has the faintest blush on her cheeks," gasped Jario.

Laralynn's pale cheeks had begun to change to a soft peach, and her lips had replaced their blue hue with a soft rose color. As her hair began to brighten to the fiery reddish-copper he loved, he felt Jario slap him on the shoulder.

"You did it, Baxter. You brought her back."

They both watched and waited for her to open her eyes, but she kept them closed. It was the sound of air passing through her slightly parted lips that assured Baxter she had returned, and told him it was time to pull the shard from her heart.

Baxter stood and pushed the stool away and looked to Jario for an encouraging word.

"You've not turned a human before, have you?" asked Jario.

"No."

"I've killed more than I have turned, but I can help you through it."

"When I pull the shard from her heart, she will fill this cot with blood. I need to move her to the floor. It will save this cot for her recovery."

Jario agreed and helped Baxter move her to the floor.

"Before we begin, I need to remove her clothes so she has something to wear when she awakens."

"I think that is something you can do on your own. I'm sure she would not take kindly to me helping you undress her. I'll go sit at the table and skin the rest of those rabbits. If you need my help, you know where to find me."

Trying to keep his eyes focused on anything but her naked body, he managed to remove her clothes and also preserve her dignity. With the coverlet pulled up against the shard, he turned to Jario.

"When do I offer her my wrist?"

"Just before her heart stops beating," replied Jario. "You must give her your blood just before her heart stops beating, or she will be lost to you forever."

Baxter released a nervous sigh and nodded at Jario.

"I'm ready to start."

"Place your fingers on the side of her throat. You should be able to feel the beat of her heart."

He did as he was told, and when he found her heart's gentle pulse, he looked at Jario seeking further instructions.

"Now, slowly pull the shard from her heart. Be prepared; she may cry out in pain, but don't stop."

Baxter felt his jaw tighten as he gripped what remained of the shard of ice. He closed his eyes and slowly pulled it upward. When it began to move, he felt her body stiffen, and a groan passed from her lips. As the shard's tip passed cleanly from her heart, he saw her life's blood begin to flow from the open wound. Laralynn was dying.

The beat of her heart began to slow until it was almost undetectable. Lifting his wrist to his mouth, he let his fangs descend and tore at his wrist. Pressing his thumb against her chin, he drew her mouth open and placed his wrist at her mouth letting his blood drip against her tongue. It was then that he noticed a single tear had fallen across her cheek. It was a moment of sadness he would never forget.

After washing the blood from her body and dressing her in her tunic, Baxter gently lifted her limp body from the floor and carried her back to the cot to sleep. With the coverlet tucked under her chin, he leaned over and kissed her forehead.

"When you wake, I hope you are able to forgive me for what I have done. Now, sleep, my love. I will be here when you wake, and we will start anew."

* * *

Baxter had watched the sun rise and set for five painfully long days. He had hunted during the day while Jario kept watch over Laralynn. When the daylight gave itself over to the darkness, Jario took to the forest to feed, while Baxter patiently sat by Laralynn's side waiting for her to wake. She had not moved, called out from a nightmare, or even shed another tear since he had given her his blood. Again, she was lost to him.

Even though Baxter was eager for Laralynn to wake, it was the days of turmoil after his turning that consumed his thoughts. He remembered the heavy shackles that had circled his wrists when he sat in the Holding Room at Evergreen. He had felt uncontrollable anger swirling in his mind, and his throat constantly burned for the taste of blood; however, it was the need to escape that drove him mad.

As Baxter looked about the cottage, he knew they would be unable to restrain her. If she escaped the cottage, the sunlight could turn her to ash.

Must I bind myself to you to keep you safe, Laralynn?

Baxter started to laugh. He suddenly remembered the shackles he wore were spelled by the witch, Meadow. Had they not been spelled, he would have broken free and escaped his prison.

A mere binding would serve no purpose, he thought. For, she would be strong enough to break them. How foolish for me to think, otherwise?

Remembering the Sentries, he suddenly feared what it would mean if Topaz allowed them to wake. They would all be without their gifts and prisoners to the darkness until they could figure out a way to escape. They needed the Sentries to remain sleeping.

"Baxter, are you there?" called a voice he had dreaded hearing since they had fallen into Alabaster.

"My Lady, I hear you," replied Baxter."

"I know there is trouble. I can feel it. Do not try to hide it from me," replied Lara. "I have tried to reach my daughter, and her mind shows me nothing but darkness. I sent you back to Wintergreen Mountain to bring her to Evergreen. You did not return. What has happened?"

"We fell through the ice and through a portal to a place called Alabaster. In doing so, we lost the use of our gifts, and Laralynn was badly injured. A shard of ice pierced her heart, and Queen Nora's healers were caring for her."

"What do you mean they were caring for her? If she needs healing, you must bring her back to Evergreen."

"There is too much to explain, My Lady. I beg you to read my mind and discover what has happened. When we are able to return, I will accept your punishment and leave Evergreen if that is your will."

Baxter closed his eyes and willingly gave his mind over to Lady Lara. He could feel the moment she entered his mind, and he waited for her stern response.

"I know all that you have seen and heard. I am not pleased with the bargain you have made with the traitor, Jario. I fear he will not honor the bargain, and in the end, he will return to Alltree for revenge. However, I am proud of the pledge you have made to Queen Nora. She needs your help and so do her people. We know very well the ways of a traitor, and the turmoil it can cause a kingdom."

"I am sorry, My Lady. I did what I thought best to help Laralynn."

"Do not let your mind carry the heavy burden of her turning. I have seen her daydream while sitting by the fountain in our courtyard and have read her thoughts. She has secretly wished to become a vampire."

"Laralynn has confided in me of her desire to be like me."

"Now that she will be, I fear what will happen when she wakes. She is unprepared for the transition from human to vampire and knows nothing of the temptations that will follow."

"That is my concern, as well."

"I advise you to use your gift of compulsion to keep her under control and hope she hasn't been given the gift to block it. In the meantime, I will speak with Meadow. She may be able to help us."

"Thank you, My Lady."

"I must go. Take care of my daughter and Queen Nora the best you can. I trust your judgment, Baxter."

"I will do my best, My Lady."

She was gone from his mind as quickly as she had entered it. He had made choices that clearly disappointed her, but there was no talk of punishment or banishment. With that knowledge, he was greatly relieved. One thing was certain; Lady Lara wanted him to defend Queen Nora, but how? He was too far away to be of any help, and he couldn't leave Laralynn.

Uncertain if it would work, he tried to find a path to Queen Nora's mind. He could feel a cold shiver race down his back as his search brushed against a tunnel covered in frost. Further and further he traveled until he reached a wall of ice. Her mind was blocked. Was it by her own doing or had it been protected by the Sentries? Not knowing if his intrusion would be forgiven, he shattered the ice and found himself surrounded by Queen Nora's thoughts.

"Queen Nora, it's Baxter. I feel your sadness. Has something happened?"

Nora looked about her bedchamber for Baxter. She had clearly heard his voice, but she could not see him.

"My door is bolted," she gasped. *"How have you managed to enter my bedchamber? Step out from your hiding place so that I may see you."*

"I still sit within the cottage with the Lady Laralynn. I have not left the Floating Forest. I speak to your mind, and I ask your forgiveness for the intrusion."

Feeling the room beginning to spin, Nora sank down upon the bench at the foot of her bed. Leaning over, she held her head in her hands. Breathing deeply, she tried to calm herself.

"I am not sure I believe what I am hearing."

"Is it fair to say a man should believe his eyes when a woman turns into a lioness or a man into a lion? If so, why would it be so hard to believe that you could hear my voice in your mind?"

"No, it is not too much to believe. You merely took me by surprise. It is the first time someone has invaded my mind. I always thought my thoughts to be my own and protected by a shield of ice."

"I promise to tread lightly, My Queen. Now, tell me what has happened since we left the dungeon?"

"Much has changed. Vitas discovered your cells were empty, and the guard has been sentenced to death for treason. Crew ordered Teppo and Satu removed from the Healing Room, and they have been hidden within the many rooms of the tower. I have not been allowed to see them and have been confined to my bedchamber until I bow to King Crew."

"Have they harmed you?"

"No."

"Has any harm come to Topaz or Ruby?"

"No, Vitas fears their powers, and he is still unaware of the sleeping Sentries."

"And, where does Vitas believe we have gone? Is he searching for us?"

"He believes you have been hiding within the castle since your escape and has his army searching for you."

"Does he know of the portal to the Floating Forest? Would he send his army here to search for us?"

"He knows of it, but he fears it. Satu told tales of horned creatures in the forest upon his return, and Vitas is not brave enough to lead them through the portal."

"Creatures, you made no mention of creatures?"

"Satu's horned creatures were nothing more than his exaggerated tales of glory to prove his manhood, and I let Vitas think it to be true. If you look, you will find the creatures from his tales. Deer and boar freely roam the forest. You need not fear Vitas' arrival. He is consumed with his puppet king."

"I am sorry for the trouble we have caused you and your people."

"It is clear to me now that Vitas would have seen to Teppo's demise at

some point. He is hungry for power and cares little for the people of Alabaster."

"Then, we shall take steps to remove him."

"How? Is Laralynn well?"

"Sadly, she is still sleeping, but she has returned to her body. I have pulled the shard from her heart and fed her my blood. It is only a matter of time before she wakes. Once her desires of the blood are under control, we will return to help you remove Vitas from Alabaster."

"Hurry, I'm not sure how long it will be before I find myself in Alabaster's dungeon."

"I promise you, My Queen, we will come as soon as we are able. I will contact you again when we are ready to join you."

"I eagerly await your arrival."

Chapter 16

Awakened

Laralynn's scream jolted Baxter and Jario from their sleep. They rushed to her side and found her sitting straight-up clutching the worn coverlet to her chest with tears streaming from her eyes.

"I can't see. The light is too bright," cried Laralynn. "What's happened to my eyes?"

Baxter sat down on the edge of the cot and wrapped his arms around her. With her head against his chest, he gently rocked her until her tearful sobbing calmed to a meek whimper.

"Don't cry, Laralynn. You have been in the darkness much too long. You're going to be well soon," Baxter whispered, trying to reassure her. "What do you remember?"

"I remember drifting down through the icy water and the sound of something shattering. The sound woke me from a dream of a faceless man searching for my magical sword. When I opened my eyes, I was floating in a dark sky filled with bright, beautiful stars, and someone was calling my name. Was it you, Baxter?"

"Yes, I called your name. I was afraid I had lost you."

Jario could see that Laralynn's eyes were now open, but she was looking down at the floor. He knelt next to the cot, and as he did, she looked directly at him.

"Look at her eyes, Baxter. Her eyes have changed. They're lavender," he gasped, as he stood and stepped away from the cot. "That isn't the way it is supposed to work. Her eyes should be red."

"Laralynn, look at me. Let me see your eyes," demanded Baxter.

As she raised her face toward his, he could see lavender eyes staring back at him. They were rimmed in dark blue and sprinkled with flecks of silver. To him, they were much more beautiful than the red he expected.

"Can you see me?" asked Baxter.

"Yes, I see the worried look on your face," she laughed. "My eyes no longer hurt. It is just as you said; I must have been in the dark too long."

"Why are her eyes not red?" asked Jario. "Her eyes should be red."

"Why should my eyes be red, or better yet, why are my eyes lavender?" she asked. Looking again at Jario, she scowled. "Wait, why is Jario here with us?"

"There are some things I need to tell you," sighed Baxter. "I would rather tell you in private."

"I can see that I'm not wanted. I'll leave the two of you alone," said Jario as he turned toward the door. "I'll go hunting. After all, we'll all need to feed."

As the cottage door closed, Baxter took hold of Laralynn's hands and nervously rubbed his thumbs against her fingers.

"Please let me tell you everything before you speak."

Laralynn offered him a timid smile and nodded for him to continue.

"The shattering you heard was you falling through a portal to a place called Alabaster. We all fell through the same portal, but you were badly injured. A shard of ice pierced your heart."

Laralynn pulled her hand free from his and touched the place where the shard had been.

"Your wound was so severe; I knew there was only one way to save you. I tried to flash you back to Evergreen, but my gifts were gone. There was nothing I could do to save us," sighed Baxter. "We were arrested by the Alabaster guards, and you were taken to the Queen's Healing Room. Later, we discovered the Sentries' magic guarded the portal, and they had removed our gifts to protect the people of Alabaster. Eventually, Jario and I were brought before the king. He wanted to know who we were and why we had come. I explained our orders were to arrest Jario for his crimes against Evergreen, and he sent Jario to the dungeon."

"But, he is with us. Why is he with us?" she asked.

"Let me finish. You must know all of it."

"Continue."

"I was allowed to stay with you in the Healing Room until the king and his son fell ill. We were all blamed for his illness by Commander Vitas and taken to the dungeon. The queen learned of a plot to take the king's throne, and she helped devise a plan for us to escape. One of the healers made the Sentries sleep so that we could regain our gifts. The queen brought me to a place she calls the *Floating Forest*, and this is where we are now. This is where I removed the shard and watched your life fade away until I fed you my blood."

Baxter shifted on the cot and found he could no longer look at her. He couldn't bring himself to tell her she was a vampire. He felt ashamed that he was unable to keep her from harm.

"You forget, my love, that I can read your thoughts, and they have shown me what has happened to me. You must not feel bad, for you are not to blame for my misfortune. I stepped out onto the ice, and I didn't follow you back to Evergreen. I put myself in danger. I have seen all of it, and I know I was dying. You saved me the only way you could. For that, I am grateful."

"You aren't angry?"

"Why should I be angry? You gave me the gift of life. Without it, I would be alone in the Otherworld. Instead, I can live forever with you."

"I am surprised you are so calm. When I woke after being turned, I was filled with rage and the need for blood."

"I feel just the same as I did before we found Jario on the ice. There is no feeling of rage or a desire for blood."

Baxter noticed the sun was beginning to rise and expected Jario to return at any moment. He stood and made his way to the window. Pulling back the fabric, he exposed the leaded panes.

"Come stand by me. We need to know if the sunlight will harm you."

"You want to risk letting the sun burn my skin? Is there no other way?"

"If we were at Evergreen, I would take you to the Room of Powers, and you could see the Wispet Queen one more time, but we aren't there."

"Then, take me back to Evergreen. Your gifts have been returned to you. There is no reason we can't leave this place and Jario behind."

"There is a reason, Laralynn. I promised Queen Nora that I would not return to Evergreen until King Teppo and Satu have been healed. I will honor my promise. The people of Alabaster need our help. If the king is healed, he will be able to remove his brother from the throne, charge Vitas with treason, and take back his kingdom."

"Once that is done, will we be free to leave?"

"Yes."

Ready to help fulfill Baxter's promise, Laralynn quickly pushed the coverlet from her bare legs. Confused, she looked up at Baxter's sheepish grin.

"Baxter, where are my clothes?"

"They were torn and blood stained from the fall. The healers removed them once you were taken to the Queen's Healing Room."

"Did you bring me here like this? I am half naked."

"No, the healers dressed you before we were taken to the dungeon."

"I was dressed before I was taken to the dungeon, but now, I am half naked. Why, Baxter?"

He looked at the floor not wanting to face Laralynn' anger.

"I removed your clothes before I removed the shard from your heart. If I hadn't, they would have been covered in your blood. Please know that I did my best to preserve your modesty. You must believe me. They were removed for no other purpose. Once the blood was washed away, I pulled the tunic over your head and laid your head upon the pillow to sleep. The rest I left for you to do on your own."

"I see, and where are my breeches, now?" she asked, trying to keep from laughing as he fidgeted before her.

"I put them under your pillow."

He saw her lift the pillow, withdraw her breeches, and hold them up over her head.

"I'll turn around and give you some privacy."

He heard the rustling of fabric, the sound of her bare feet on the floor, and then the feel of her arms around his waist. Turning to face her, he leaned in and gently kissed her lips. It was then that he noticed the scent of fresh apples and a surge of heat racing up his arms.

"Did you feel that?" he asked.

"You felt it too?"

"You have come back to me. Everything is how it was before."

"Almost everything."

The door swung open and in walked Jario with rabbits flung over his shoulder.

"I figured she would be hungry," grinned Jario. "Shall we drink a little blood to toast the new vampire?"

"That sounds disgusting," snapped Laralynn. "I have no desire for rabbit blood or to drink with a traitor."

"Let's keep things civil, Laralynn. He has helped me care for you, and in return for his help, I will be taking him back to the Isle of Flames."

"You what?" yelled Laralynn. "We have been ordered to arrest him and take him to Evergreen to face his final death. You would disobey your orders?"

"I will deal with the ramifications of my decisions when I return to Evergreen. For now, we have more pressing matters. We need to know a few things about you before we make our way to Alabaster. Can you walk in sunlight, and do you need blood?"

Jario dropped all but one of the rabbits on the table. With the flick of his wrist, he had torn the rabbit's head from its body. Blood ran down over his hand as he offered the rabbit's body to Laralynn.

"Care for a taste?" he smirked. "It's fresh."

"That's disgusting. Get that away from me."

"Are you saying that you feel no desire to taste the blood?" asked Baxter.

"I want no part of it."

Baxter stepped away from Laralynn and lifted his wrist to his mouth. Letting his fangs descend, he scraped them across his wrist until blood began to run from the wound. Taking a step toward Laralynn, he lifted his wrist to her mouth and watched her turn her head.

"I said I want no part of it. Remove your wrist from my face," she demanded.

"This can't be. I have known of no vampire that refuses blood, especially right after being turned," choked Jario. "She will go mad without it."

"It must be a gift. There is no other explanation," declared Baxter. "She is like no other vampire. She is truly special."

Seeing the pool of light upon the wooden floor, Baxter looked at Laralynn and beckoned her to move toward it.

"We need to know if you can survive in the sunlight. If you can't, we'll know very soon. Place you hand in the light. If it starts to burn, pull it back as quickly as you can."

She stepped toward the ray of light that streamed against the floor. Lifting her hand, she inched it forward until the tips of her fingers were covered by the light. She felt nothing. Unsure that she had done it properly, she let the light cover her hand completely. It wasn't pain she felt, but Baxter's embrace that stunned her.

"You didn't burn," he whispered into her hair. "My love, you have the gift. You can walk in daylight."

Chapter 17

Return to Alabaster

Baxter felt Laralynn was finally prepared to return to Alabaster. She had faced three sunrises without any desire for blood or ill effects from the sunlight. She was able to flash, read thoughts, and had even practiced her *gift of truth* with Jario. The time had come to contact Queen Nora and make their way back to Alabaster's castle.

Laralynn sat cross-legged on the floor facing Baxter. She took hold of his hands and closed her eyes as she waited for Baxter to call the queen. Baxter opened his mind to Laralynn and felt her gentle, reassuring presence as he started his search back through the portal and frost covered tunnel to Alabaster.

"Queen Nora, are you there? Can you hear me?"

"I hear you. Is all well with Lady Laralynn? Are you ready to come help me?"

"We are ready, My Queen."

"I have warned Topaz that you could appear unexpectedly, and she has assured me that she will wait for you."

"I will contact you, again, once we have arrived."

"I wish you good luck."

Without hesitation, Baxter broke the connection.

"It's time to go. We are headed for the Healing Room. I am told that Topaz will be waiting for us. Jario, we will need you to hide us with your haze. If Topaz is alone, it will be safe to show ourselves."

As they held each other's hands, Jario covered them with his haze, and Baxter flashed them from the cottage. A single candle offered just enough light to see that Topaz was alone and to keep them hidden in the shadows from prying eyes.

"I know you are here," offered Topaz. "I am alone. You may show yourselves."

Jario released his haze, and they stepped from the shadows.

"Can you take us to the king?" asked Baxter.

"King Teppo is in the tower and well-guarded by those that are faithful to Commander Vitas. He has chosen five of the largest and fiercest of the lions to stand guard," replied Topaz.

"Do they possess special gifts or have the use of magic?" asked Baxter.

"Once they have shifted to their lion form, they have enhanced senses. They will hear you coming and be able to track you by your scent, even if you are hidden from view. Their paws are deadly. Do not allow them to scratch you, for if they do, their poison will cause paralysis. You will be unable to hear or speak. Illness will consume your body, and eventually, you will succumb to death."

"Three against five, it could be worse," joked Laralynn.

"Can you lead us to the tower?" asked Baxter.

"Vitas has forbidden me passage to anywhere except my bedchamber, the Healing Room, and the queen's bedchamber. If you can hide me as you have done yourselves, I can lead you to the stone steps. We will pass the queen's bedchamber on the way."

"We'll follow you to the queen's bedchamber. Once there, Jario will cover you with his haze, and you can lead us to the tower steps. Then, Laralynn will flash you back to the Healing Room to keep you out of danger. Are you ready?"

"Yes."

* * *

Topaz moved quickly through the hallways with the threesome close on her heels. As she made the last turn before reaching the queen's door, Jario saw Crew and two guards coming toward them.

"Stand flat against the wall. Trouble is headed our way," whispered Jario.

They tightened their bodies against the wall as Topaz stood with her head bowed waiting for them to pass.

"Why are you not in the Healing Room?" asked Crew as he stopped his guards behind him. "Vitas has given orders for everyone to keep the halls clear."

"I am on my way to see Queen Nora. She has fallen ill and asked to see me."

"Then, be quick about it. It is not safe to roam about the hallways. We are still searching for the intruders. Until we find them, we need these hallways clear."

"I will, My King."

With a smirk upon his face, Crew waved his hand, and the guards quickly followed after him.

Fearing what Crew would do if he returned to find her still in the hallway, she scurried off toward the guard that stood before the queen's door.

"I'm here to see the queen."

"On whose orders?" asked the guard.

"Crew knows that I am here to see the queen. He told me to be quick about it."

"I was not told anything about this."

"Do you want me to bring Crew here so that you may ask him?"

The guard shook his head and pulled the keys from his belt. He unlocked the door and pushed it open allowing Topaz to enter with Laralynn and Baxter quick to follow her. After pulling the door closed, he turned to stand in front of the door, but instead, he was confronted by Jario.

"What's this?" blurted the guard.

Using his gift of compulsion, Jario looked directly into the guard's eyes and said, "You will do as I say without making a sound. You will stand guard beside the queen's door and forget that you have seen me. If questioned about the queen, you will say that she is safe and has been sleeping. You will remember Topaz came to visit the queen and that she left to return to the Healing Room. Now, do as I have commanded."

Without a response, the guard took his position beside the door, and Jario entered the chamber to find Baxter alone with Queen Nora.

"Where is Laralynn?" asked Jario.

"She has taken Topaz back to the Healing Room. The queen will guide us to the tower. If we find the king and Laralynn can wake him, the queen will be the only person that he will trust."

"You risk the queen's life by bringing her with us," cautioned Jario.

"It is a risk I am willing to take," declared Nora. "Teppo would do the same for me. I can do no less for him."

Baxter had caught Laralynn's scent before he felt her take his hand, and he was relieved to have her safe by his side.

"Before we move forward, let me remind all of you of what Topaz warned us about the lions. Laralynn, if you are scratched, flash back to the cottage before the paralysis affects you. If you don't, it will distract the rest of us from our goal," ordered Baxter. "Jario, do your best to keep us covered with your haze as long as you can. If you fall, one of us will try to flash you to safety."

"If a lion is lucky enough to scratch me, he will regret it," laughed Jario. "I still have my gift of stone, and I won't hesitate to use it."

"Before we go, I need to tell you that I am proud to be beside such brave warriors," sighed Nora. "If you are faced with a choice to save the king or me, I ask that you save the king. He will put an end to those that committed this act of treason and see that our people are protected."

"We will save you both," replied Laralynn. "I know a king is nothing without his queen. Now, let's stop being so sentimental and find the king."

* * *

They had all managed to reach the foot of the stone steps undetected and appointed Jario to lead them up the stairwell since his gift of stone was the most damaging. It was vital to reach the landing at the top of the steps before anyone else had need of the stairwell. For, it was too narrow for two people to pass each other easily and would surely cause them to be discovered.

With a hand touching the back of the person ahead of them, they quietly and cautiously took one step at a time until the landing was one step away from Jario. He could hear talking and stopped. Everyone felt the abrupt halt and waited for Jario to allow them to continue. Still covered in his haze, he peered around the corner to see three guards in human form. He could see four open doors and the flicker of candlelight coming from another stairwell. He moved his hand behind his back and touched Baxter's hand. When he felt Baxter grip his hand, he displayed three fingers and hoped he would know what it meant. Baxter responded by scraping his fingernails against Jario's palm. Confused at first, it took a moment for Jario to understand Baxter's question. He closed his fist to say no. They weren't lions.

Baxter nudged Jario forward keeping his hand resting on his back, and Laralynn followed. Walking quietly toward the guards, Laralynn peered into each room and found them empty. The king wasn't on this floor. Hearing a muffled cough, she turned to see a guard slump to the floor. As the two other guards reached for him, they suddenly turned to stone.

"Get Queen Nora, we need to keep moving," Baxter said into Laralynn's mind.

As quietly as she could, she retrieved the queen and stood ready at the next stairwell. Once they had started to climb the steps, Jario dropped his haze.

"What are you doing?" whispered Baxter.

"It's too hard to communicate with it," he replied. "I'll throw it back up if I hear anyone coming our way."

Baxter nodded, and they kept moving until they reached the next landing. Again, Jario pulled his haze and peered around the corner. Two huge lions stood guard outside a closed door. Two doors were open, but the rooms were dark. The stairwell to the next floor was dark, as well. He knew the king had to be on this floor.

Jario drew back, dropping his haze, and turned to face Baxter. He raised two fingers on his right hand and then made a claw with his fingers. Everyone knew what it meant. Jario had seen two lions. He then raised his hands over his head making a ring with his fingers and saw Nora draw her hand to her mouth to stifle a gasp. He pressed his finger to his lips to remind everyone to be quiet. If they had any chance of saving the king, they had to stay quiet.

Baxter looked at Jario and tilted his head while shrugging his shoulders. They had to strike now or risk the lions finding them. Jario nodded, pulled his haze to cover everyone, and stepped up onto the landing. He saw the lions immediately turn their heads and flick their tails. Standing frozen in place, he waited for Baxter to make the last step to join him.

The lions looked agitated and began pacing in a circle. The closed door opened and out walked Vitas. If he headed for the stairwell, he would surely discover Laralynn and Queen Nora. Baxter waited and watched for any sign that Vitas was leaving.

"Teppo and his son are still asleep. I am going to check on the queen. I hear she has become ill. We may be lucky enough to rid Alabaster of all of them," laughed Vitas.

Baxter flinched as he felt a hand brush against his back. He was sure Laralynn had heard Vitas and moved Nora from the stairwell.

"I can see into the chamber. When he closes the door, I'm going to flash the queen behind its door," Laralynn spoke into Baxter's mind. *"You*

heard him. He is going to check on the queen. We have very little time to keep her safe."

"Take her to the cottage," he replied. "I'll see to the king and his son."

Vitas closed the door and headed toward the stairwell, while the lions still paced in circles.

"No one is to enter that chamber," ordered Vitas. "They will forfeit their life if they do."

The lions roared in acknowledgment.

Baxter knew the moment Laralynn had vanished, for the heat he had felt from her closeness had vanished as well. Letting her slip from his mind, he was now free to focus on saving the king. He reached for Jario and found his arm. Gripping it tightly, he flashed inside the chamber.

Seeing only the king and his son spread out on long narrow tables, Jario dropped his haze.

"I'm going to flash us all back to the cottage," whispered Baxter.

"Where are Laralynn and the queen?" asked Jario.

"She has already taken the queen to the cottage."

"Now, take Satu's hand and hold on as tight as you can. I'm taking us out of here."

Baxter stepped between the two sleeping men and took hold of the king's hand. As he reached for Satu, he felt something sharp rip the flesh from his back. A lion had been resting under the king's table and now stood behind Baxter's bleeding back.

"Flash, don't wait!" yelled Jario as he pulled his haze to cover them. He crouched under Satu's table and reached for Baxter. Finding the sleeve of his tunic, he began pulling him away from the lion.

A loud crack sounded as the two lion guards burst through the door. Smelling the blood, they were drawn to where Baxter had lain sprawled on the floor. The lion that had attacked Baxter stood squarely between the two tables forcing the other lions to circle around to the other side.

Jario could feel Baxter's body go limp, and he knew it was just a matter of time before the lions found them.

"Stay away from them!" screamed Laralynn.

Jario crawled out from under the table to see Laralynn standing in the corner with her hands held out in front of her. Her hands were engulfed in flames. Fearing the lions had used some magic against her, he ran toward the lions. He hurled himself against the lion's back closest to him and pulled his gift of stone. After seeing the lion turned to stone, the other lions backed away giving Jario enough time to pull Laralynn from the corner.

"Where is he?" she gasped.

Jario dropped his haze and pointed to the space under the table.

"Keep them away from us while I get Baxter. We're leaving this place," she yelled.

Jario held off the lions while Laralynn pulled Baxter from the floor and laid him beside Satu. She took hold of the king's hand and then grasped Baxter's.

"Jario, come quickly. Take Satu's hand and grasp my arm. Whatever you do, don't let go."

He did as she asked, and they vanished just as Vitas entered the chamber.

Chapter 18

Healing

It had been four days since Laralynn had brought everyone to safety and collapsed on the cottage floor from exhaustion. She had slept for two days and cried for the better part of one after seeing Baxter's mauled and paralyzed body. There had been no mention of the fire that engulfed her hands by Laralynn, and Jario thought it best to stay silent. He had remembered that Magna had acquired the ability to change her appearance from drinking his blood, and he assumed Baxter's blood had been the reason for the flames she had brandished. Due to Laralynn's fragile state, he had decided to wait until she was ready to speak of it, and he wondered what other gifts she had acquired from Baxter's blood.

After two more days of silence, she was finally able to deal with what had happened to Baxter and ready to put her healing hands to work.

"Jario, I need fresh water. The cleanest water you can find. My healing gift only seems to work with water. Can you fetch it for me?" asked Laralynn.

He nodded and reached for the bucket, for he was willing to do anything that would help get him on his way to Firelight Castle.

"Queen Nora, are you hungry? Do you need Jario to hunt?"

asked Laralynn.

"I am hungry, but I can go into the forest with Jario. I can shift and hunt while he finds water. I know these forests and can easily find my way back to the cottage."

"No, you stay here and help Laralynn. I'll find something for the hearth that will be enough for all of us. Besides, I need to feed," explained Jario. With the bucket in one hand and a hatchet in the other, he turned and quickly left the cottage.

Nora had been curious about the change she had seen in Jario since he stood before Teppo confessing his crimes. He had been both brave and protective when confronted by the guards and the lions. She had seen him clean Baxter's wounds and keep a watchful eye on Laralynn as she slept. He did not seem to be a danger to anyone, and she had to know why.

"I know that you and Baxter were sent to arrest Jario, but he seems to have changed from the traitor that stood before Teppo," stated Nora. "I'm sure you have seen it too. Will he be shown any mercy for his good deeds?"

Laralynn laughed to herself. She had seen the change and appreciated his new behavior, but she knew it was only temporary. Once he was free, he would eagerly return to his wicked way of living. His need for power was far greater than his need to do good.

"Don't be fooled by his smile or his good deeds. He is a dangerous vampire, and he has betrayed everyone at Evergreen, including me. He can change his mind as easily as he can change his appearance. It will be up to my mother to determine his fate. She will know if he has truly changed. If he has, she will show him mercy, but if not, he will be given a traitor's death. That is if Baxter doesn't take him to the Isle of Flames."

"Why does he want to go there so badly?"

"Mistress Violeta commanded him to bring her the *Singing Sword*. He came back to Alltree Island and stole it from a hidden chamber in Black Thistle Castle. We were ordered to retrieve the sword and arrest him for the crime. It wasn't easy, but we found Jario hiding on a frozen lake on Wintergreen Mountain with the sword in hand. We had him in our grasp when the ice began to crack. The sword was in his possession when we fell through the ice and then through the portal. If Jario was able to retrieve the sword after the fall, I can only assume the guards took it from him. Trust me. His thoughts are only of that sword and his well-being. If he doesn't return the sword to Mistress Violeta within nine moons, he will die a final death."

"I understand; she has given him no choice but to obey her command. Is Baxter forced to obey her command, as well?"

"No, Baxter made a bargain with Jario. In return for helping to keep me safe and putting Teppo back on the throne, he promised he would see Jario safely to the island. As far as I know, Jario has kept his part of the bargain. In return, Baxter will keep his word and deliver him to Mistress Violeta."

"You have been through so much since coming through the portal to Alabaster. I am truly sorry for the pain it has caused you and Baxter. I hope you will not judge us all by Vitas' betrayal."

"What is done can't be changed," sighed Laralynn. "I only hope my healing gift will set things right for the king, your son, and for Baxter."

"As do I, Laralynn, as do I."

"I have talked enough about Jario. It would please me if we could talk about something else."

Nora stood from Teppo's cot and made her way to the table. She pulled the small bench out from under the table and sat down. Placing her hand on the space next to her, she patted it with her fingers hoping Laralynn would sit down beside her. Laralynn complied, and Nora took her hand in her own.

"Please call me Nora, for we are well beyond formalities." Seeing Laralynn's smile eased her nervous mind. "Tell me about what lies beyond the portal. It has been a very long time since I have gone through the barrier. I remember little of my visit, and what I do remember has surely changed by now."

"You've gone through the portal?"

"I have only passed through the portal twice, once to leave

Alabaster and once to return. My mother and father took me through the portal to a place far from the ice and snow of Alabaster. The sun was warm on my face, and I remember the scents of pine, lavender, and the salty air of the sea. We visited a castle with tall towers that overlooked the darkest blue water I had ever seen. I had forgotten the visit until I saw the emblem upon your tunic. The banners that hung upon the stone walls of that castle held the same emblem."

"My stars, you were at Evergreen Castle," gasped Laralynn. "Do you remember anyone?"

"While my parents discussed important matters, I played within the castle walls with two girls much younger than myself. Their names were Lara and Magna."

"I can't believe it," cried Laralynn. "Lara is my mother. You played with my mother. What was she like?"

"It was so long ago, and I don't remember much. I do remember that Magna was very shy, and Lara always held her hand. When we left, Lara gave me a ribbon from her hair as a memento of our visit. I believe I still have it in my treasure box."

"Why have you never returned?"

"Our world is far removed from your world, and there was never a reason to leave Alabaster."

"Well, when all of this unrest is settled, I hope you will find a reason to visit Evergreen. I'm sure my mother would enjoy seeing you again."

"I would like that very much."

The door opened, and Jario entered carrying a bucket of water in one hand and three pigeons in the other. Tucked under his arm were a bunch of wild onions, his hatchet, and a branch covered in bright red berries. After setting the bucket on the floor, he laid the rest of his bounty on the table.

"If you pour the water into the cooking pot, I'll retrieve more for you to use for the healing. I found a waterfall not far from the cottage, and I can bring you all the water you need."

Laralynn nodded and did as he asked. As she returned the

bucket, she offered her thanks and watched him hurry from the cottage.

* * *

Even though Nora desperately wanted Teppo to be healed first, she understood Laralynn's reasoning for wanting to heal Baxter. She knew that Laralynn feared the arrival of Vitas and his guards, and secretly, she did as well. He would eventually set his fear of Satu's creatures aside for his need to find the king and those he called the intruders. They had embarrassed him in front of his guards, and he would want his revenge. His revenge would be an agonizing death for everyone, including herself.

The time had come for Laralynn to try and heal Baxter. She sat on the edge of the cot and began removing the strips of cloth Jario had torn from Nora's gauzy under-slip to cover Baxter's wounds. Stiff with dried blood and smelling of infection, she dropped them into a basket by the bed. Knowing he had placed maggots in the gashes to eat away the infected skin had already made her queasy, but the sight of them quickly brought a foul, bitter taste to the back of her throat. Holding her hand over her mouth, she felt herself gag in response.

"You'll be fine, child. Focus your mind on healing him," Nora whispered, as she rubbed circles at the base of Laralynn's neck.

Closing her eyes for a moment to clear her mind, she slowly opened her eyes and forced herself to see only his ravaged back. One by one, she removed the maggots from his wounds, and with Nora's help, they washed the remaining bits of dead flesh away.

Even clean, his back was a horrible sight to behold. There were five deep gashes across his back, and the deepest and most severe were near his shoulder. They were fiery-red with swollen lumps that oozed a rancid yellowish liquid. His arm had fared better than his back, for Baxter must have been able to turn away from the lion's claws. In doing so, they had merely scratched his arm leaving only bright red streaks behind.

Jario had poured the water from the bucket into a pitcher to make it easier for Nora to hold and pour the water into Laralynn's hands. He stood ready with the bucket to offer more when the pitcher was empty and near enough to watch Laralynn. He had never seen her use her gift of healing and was eager to watch her work.

"I am ready to begin, Nora." She held her hands together and curved her fingers forming the shape of a cup. "Slowly pour some water into my hands. I will start with his arm since it is the least damaged."

Nora held the pitcher by the handle and placed her other hand under the spout for support. Slowly tipping the spout down, she allowed a small stream of water to fill Laralynn's hands partially. Taking a step back, she watched as Laralynn let the water run from her hands over Baxter's arm. The marks instantly began to fade.

"It's working," gasped Jario.

As Nora began to fill Laralynn's hands again, the red marks reappeared as red as before.

"The poison is stronger than my gift of healing," muttered Laralynn. "What do I do, now?"

"I don't believe it is stronger, Laralynn. I believe there is a great amount of poison in his body that must be removed," replied Nora. "Seeing you pour the water onto his arm made me think of rinsing the soap from my hair. It takes several pitchers of water to rinse my hair clean. It may be the same with the poison. This time, pour the water on the worst of his wounds. Focus the stream of water on the worst of the wounds."

Laralynn nodded and held out her hands for more water. "You remind me of my mother, Nora. You have the same calming effect on me."

With her hands full again, she let the water run from her hands onto Baxter's shoulder. They could all hear a hissing sound as the water ran through the gashes. Not waiting to see if the redness had lessened, she held her hands out for more water. Over and over, she poured water from her hands onto Baxter's wounds. Gradually the swollen edges of his wounds flattened.

It had taken a dozen buckets of water and a dozen trips to the waterfall to fill them before the fiery redness faded to merely a blush, and the gashes began to close. The bedding under Baxter's body was soaked, and so were the sleeves of Laralynn's tunic. Standing in a large puddle, she could feel the water soaking into the soft leather of her boots as she stepped toward Nora for more water.

"The gashes have closed, and the redness is finally gone, my dear," Nora said, as she placed her hand on Laralynn's palms.

"Please, just one more to be sure?" Laralynn asked. "I need to be sure it's gone."

Nora filled Laralynn's hands one last time and watched her carefully pour the water over Baxter's shoulder until her hands were empty.

"Why isn't he waking? His wounds are healed, so the poison must be gone." Laralynn looked at Nora and Jario for an answer, but Jario only shook his head not knowing what to say.

"I have no answer for you. Sadly, those that have been attacked by the poison claws of the guards have all died," replied Nora. "I know that is not what you wanted to hear, but Baxter's back has healed. He may only need sleep to regain his strength just as you did when you returned us all to the cottage."

"You're right," sighed Laralynn. "That must be it. He needs to sleep. While he does, I can try to heal the king."

"How will your healing water help Teppo or my son?" she asked. "He has no wounds."

Confused and a bit weary, Laralynn began to pace back and forth trying to figure out how she could heal Teppo and Satu.

"Let them drink the water," blurted Jario.

"What?" asked Laralynn.

"They drank something that contained poison. Let Teppo and your son drink the healing water. It should heal the inside of their body."

Nora grabbed a wooden cup from the table and handed it to Jario.

"We need your hands, Laralynn," requested Nora.

Laralynn made the same curved shape with her hands and held them over the wooden cup. As Nora poured the water into Laralynn's hands, she let it spill into the cup until it was full.

"Let them drink," Jario said, as he handed the cup to Nora.

With Jario's help, she was able to pour the water into Teppo's and then Satu's mouth. In no time at all, Teppo and Satu were sitting up, and Nora was wrapped in Teppo's arms.

Laralynn hurried to Baxter's side and called to Jario, "Will you help me turn Baxter over. I want to pour water into his mouth."

Jario did as she asked but stopped her when she moved forward with the cup of water.

"I don't believe the water will help him," he said. "It has been too long since he has fed. It is blood that he needs, not water."

"Then, let's hunt," she responded.

"There is no need to hunt. Laralynn, you have the gift of healing. That means your blood will heal him."

"What?"

"Let him drink your blood."

"How?"

Jario took her by the hand and ran his finger over her wrist.

"Let your fangs descend and pierce your wrist. As the blood begins to flow, hold it over his mouth."

"I don't know how," she cried, as she pulled away. "I've never done it."

Jario felt his fangs descend as he grabbed her wrist again. He drew her wrist to his mouth and scraped the points of his fangs against her flesh being careful not to take any of her blood."

"Now, press your wrist to his mouth before it heals."

She knelt beside Baxter and rested her wrist against Baxter's open mouth. Letting her blood run across his tongue, she waited for him to wake. She could feel her wrist begin to heal, and she lifted her wrist to Jario. Taking her wrist, he scraped his fangs against her skin once more, and she returned it to Baxter's mouth. Again, her wrist began to heal, and she raised it toward Jario.

"No," snarled Baxter as he pulled Laralynn against his body. "There is no need for more blood. I am healed."

Chapter 19

Day of Truth

When Teppo realized he was far from Alabaster and that Jario was far from the dungeon's cell, his anger caused him to shift into his lion form ready to attack. It was only from Nora's soft touch and constant sweet words that allowed him to return to his human form. Taking his hand, she beckoned him and Satu to follow her outside, for she had much to tell them.

"That was too close for my liking," sighed Jario. "I think I'll put some distance between us. I'm going hunting."

He opened the door enough to see if it was safe to leave.

"Don't stay gone too long. I'm not sure when we will leave for Alabaster," Baxter cautioned. "When the time is right, I won't go looking for you."

Jario pointed to his head, "Find me when it is time. I have no fondness for lions."

With the sound of the door closing, they were finally alone. Laralynn leaned back against Baxter's chest as they sat by the warm flames of the hearth. Nothing pleased her more than the feel of his arms wrapped around her with his face nestled next to her own. She had only heard Baxter whisper a few words of affection in her ear when a ferocious roar shook the cottage causing bits of thatching to float to the floor.

"She must have told him about Vitas and the poison,"

laughed Laralynn. "He doesn't sound pleased."

"We won't be alone for long. I can hear the king walking toward the door."

Laralynn quickly stood and pulled Baxter to his feet.

"He's growling. I hope that's a good sign," she whispered, hoping Teppo couldn't hear her.

The door opened, and Teppo waited for Nora to enter before he stepped into the room. He scanned the small space looking for Jario. Not finding him, he asked, "Where is the vampire, Jario?"

"He has gone hunting. As you can imagine, he was uncomfortable," replied Baxter. "If he is needed, I can call for his return."

"Before we discuss a plan to go back to Alabaster and take back my throne, I must thank you for saving my Nora, and healing my son, and myself. Nora has told me of Vitas' plot to take my throne, the poison, and of the control he has over my brother. It saddens me to think my brother would betray me, but I have always known he is weak and easily swayed. If it were not for your help, I am sure we would have all suffered greatly."

"We are happy to see you well," offered Laralynn.

"Forgive me, I have carelessly forgotten that you were severely wounded. Nora came to me on your behalf, and I foolishly denied her request to allow the Sentries to sleep. For that, I am sorry and ask for your forgiveness."

"There is nothing to forgive," replied Laralynn. "You did what you thought best for the protection of your people."

"I did; however, it pleases me that Nora had the courage to trust you when I failed to recognize the faith she had in you." He looked down at Nora and then took her hand in his. "I am sure she will remind me of my mistake and offer her guidance in the future."

"I will indeed, my love."

"Well, I have said what I needed to say. I believe it is time to call for Jario's return. We have plans to make and traitors to send to the dungeon."

With Jario's return, a rigorous discussion concluded with the perfect plan. They would flash to the door behind the tapestry that Nora and Baxter had used for their escape. From there, they could easily make their way to the people's common area without being seen by the guards. Once there, he would be warmly greeted by his people, and no one would dare harm him.

* * *

Standing in a circle with everyone holding hands, Baxter noticed how Satu kept his eyes focused on his mother and the apprehension in the king's eyes.

"There is no need to worry. It will be quick," he assured them. "Hold tightly to the person next to you, for we will leave on the king's order."

He waited for Teppo to give the order, and it came with a quick, nervous nod of his head. Baxter squeezed Laralynn's hand, and they vanished.

Teppo seemed a little shaken when they appeared at their destination. After releasing Satu's hand, he held tightly to Nora's arm. The walls began to spin, and he dropped to his hands and knees.

"Is this dizziness common," asked Teppo. "I can't seem to make it stop."

"For some," replied Laralynn. "My father avoids flashing, for it will cause him to sleep for days. He finds traveling by horse much more to his liking."

"I understand his thinking. It will take me a moment to regain myself before I can walk among my people. I don't want them to think I am still suffering from the poison and unable to regain my throne. Vitas will surely take advantage if they see me falter."

Bending down beside Teppo, Nora lovingly stroked the side of his face and kissed his forehead, "We'll wait until you are ready, my love. No one knows we are here. No harm will come to us."

As they waited for Teppo to regain his senses, time passed slowly. He had gone from kneeling down, to leaning against the stone wall, to lying on his stomach to relieve his dizziness. Nothing seemed to work. If he stood and opened his eyes, he toppled over. It wasn't until Satu remembered Laralynn's healing gift that he pulled a small water skin from his belt.

"Will you heal my father?" asked Satu as he offered her the small pouch.

With her hands filled with water from Satu's pouch, the king lowered his head to her hands to drink. It wasn't long before his mind cleared, and he felt stable enough to stand.

"Better?" smiled Laralynn.

"Yes, I find myself much better, and I owe you my thanks, again," Teppo replied. "I am sure it looked quite undignified but well worth my embarrassment."

Nora took Teppo's arm and laughed, "I believe our undignified king is ready to see his people. Satu, will you lead the way?"

Satu opened the door and made his way to the People's Common followed by his mother and father. Jario stepped forward and stayed close to the king, as Baxter took Laralynn's hand and escorted her through the doorway.

"I want to thank you for mending my tunic. It was quite shredded, and I would have been a sight if it were not for your feminine skills," whispered Baxter.

"Feminine skills, you call it," Laralynn smirked. "In return for teaching me the bow, I will gladly teach you the skill of mending. That will teach you not to turn your back on the claws of a lion."

"As you wish, my love," he laughed. "As you wish."

The sound of chatter and laughter filled the air, as the people hurried about their day. A few gasps caught everyone's attention, and then, King Teppo's people began to kneel with their heads bowed. A young lass running toward the king broke the silence with her loud greeting. Seeing the lass, Teppo knelt to greet her.

"My King, we were told you were very ill," she said.

"I was very ill," he replied.

"My King, are you well?"

"I am well."

The lass turned to the crowd and shouted, "My King is well. My King is well."

The crowd began to cheer, and some of the women dropped their baskets to dance with the men that stood beside them. He was pleased to find his people were happy to find he had survived the poison.

"Out of my way," a voice boomed out over the crowd.

Two guards pushed people out of the way as they escorted a man wearing a long black tunic trimmed in scarlet and silver through the crowd. As they approached the king, Baxter could see it was Crew, the king's brother. Upon recognizing the king, the guards came to a sudden stop and knelt with bowed heads. Crew looked stunned to see his brother standing before him.

"Brother, no one told me you were well," choked Crew. Stepping forward, he hugged his brother for a show of friendship. "If they had, I would have greeted you properly."

'I am eager to hear of what has happened while you have cared for my throne and my people. Come, let's find Vitas. I am sure there is much to discuss," replied the king.

"Of course, My King," mumbled Crew.

* * *

Vitas stood by the warmth of his hearth holding a goblet of wine when a guard entered his chamber carrying a message. After breaking its seal, he read Crew's cryptic demand to meet him in Pride Hall. Furious, he crushed the parchment in his hand and threw it into the fire.

"How dare he demand my presence," he growled.

Storming from his chamber, he made his way through the hallways to Pride Hall. Finding the doors open, he rushed in to find Teppo sitting on his throne with Nora and Satu by his side.

Caught completely off guard, he suddenly felt a layer of doom settle over him and feared for his life. He needed to save himself, and his mind began twisting a story to implicate the king's brother as he approached his king and stood beside Crew.

"My King, it is good to find you well," Vitas nervously declared.

"Is it?" chuckled Teppo. "Let's find out just how happy you are to see me, shall we? Send in the healer, Topaz."

A guard opened a small door near the front of the hall and Topaz walked slowly toward the king.

"My dear Topaz, were you able to determine the cause of my illness?"

"My King, it was caused by poison."

"Were you able to determine who gave us the poison?"

"No, it was mixed with wine."

"And, what of my queen? Was she poisoned?"

"No, Vitas had her taken to her bedchamber. When I visited her, I found her door locked and a guard standing watch."

"It was for her protection, My King," blurted Vitas. "Nothing more."

"Quiet, you will have your turn. Topaz, you may retire to your chamber."

Topaz bowed her head and quietly left the hall.

Teppo stood and nodded toward Laralynn. Vitas looked over his shoulder to see who the king had signaled. As Laralynn stepped from the shadows, he remembered seeing the woman in the Healing Room. He saw her again in the tower for only a moment, and then she was gone.

"Now, who will tell me the truth about the poison given to my son and me? Which one of you will have the courage, to tell the truth?"

At first, neither Crew nor Vitas said a word. As the woman took her place beside the king, Vitas knew their deeds had been discovered.

"It was Crew, My King. He wanted your throne and forced

me to pour poison in your wine. He threatened to have me killed in my sleep if I did not obey him," blurted Vitas.

"Brother, he lies. It was his doing," Crew whined, and fell to his knees. "You know I am not as strong as you. I could never have done such a thing."

"So, each of you blames the other for the wicked deed. Well, I have learned of something that can help me know the truth." He reached for Laralynn's hand and helped her down the steps. "Crew, stand and step forward. Hold out your hand."

Laralynn could see the fear in his eyes and whispered, "I will not hurt you."

Crew stumbled as he stood and held out a shaking hand to Laralynn. She placed her hand upon his palm.

Teppo looked at his brother and asked, "Crew, did you pour poison in my wine?"

"No, My King," he replied.

Teppo looked at the back of Laralynn's hand and saw a blue flame appear. It was a sign that Crew was telling the truth.

"Did you devise a plot to take my throne?"

"No, My King," he said, as tears ran down his face.

The flame remained blue.

"Why did you not try to protect your king?"

"I was afraid of what Vitas would do to me if I didn't obey him."

Teppo waited to see if the flame would turn to red. It remained blue.

"You have told me the truth; however, you will be made to pay for your foolishness. I order you to live and work among the common people for 300 days. You will give up your birthright to the throne. At the end of your time among our people, you will tell me how you have made their lives better. If you cannot prove your worth to our people and me, you will be banished from Alabaster. Do you understand?"

"I do, My King. I will not fail you."

"Guards, take him away before I change my mind and send him to the dungeon."

Vitas watched as the guards led Crew away. He knew there was nothing that could save him. He had no one to blame but himself.

"Vitas, come forward and offer your hand to be judged."

"There is no need, for I am guilty of the crimes against you."

"You were my best friend. You have not only betrayed me, but you have broken my heart. For your crimes against me, I order you to receive a traitor's death. What remains of your body will burn in the Pit of Betrayal and your ashes spread far and wide. Your name will be stricken from the parchments and never be spoken by anyone at Alabaster again. Guards, remove the traitor from my sight and take him to the Traitor's Wall."

Vitas bowed his head and knelt before his king one last time. He felt the guards take his arms, and he closed his eyes as they drug him away.

Nora stood and beckoned Jario and Baxter to come forward and join them. She watched them take their place beside Laralynn, and she wondered what she would have done if they had never crashed through the portal.

"Baxter, you have fulfilled your promises to me, and for that, I will always be grateful. I think the king will allow me, this once, to speak for him. If you ever need our help, you need only ask. We will come to your aid. It will not be as payment for a favor you bestowed upon us, but as your devoted friend."

"We are honored by your kind words," replied Baxter.

"Before you go, there is the matter of your belongings. As promised, the guards will return them to you."

With their weapons returned, and the *Singing Sword* firmly tied across Jario's back, the trio stood holding each other's hands before the King and Queen of Alabaster, one last time. Nora could see a single tear fall across Laralynn's cheek, and then, they were gone from her sight.

Chapter 20

Storm and Sand

The *Withering Rose* sailed toward the Isle of Flames on calm seas every night but one. That night, everyone watched as a wicked storm filled the sky with ominous black clouds. Brilliant lightning strikes were followed by clashes of thunder, and a fierce wind blew stinging rain sideways across the deck. Small swirling funnels of rain danced across the wooden deck until they collapsed, soaking the ropes that ran between the planks. The ship's crew had seen after the fires in the galley and the lowering of the royals by the time Baxter and Jario had finished tightening all of the lashes. The ship pitched from side to side as the waves beat against its hull and lapped over the railings. The captain soon ordered the helmsman to abandon their course and sail as close to the eye of the swirling wind as possible. There was nothing left to do, but ride out the storm.

The storm had faded as quickly as it had arrived. With it finally over, Laralynn left her small cabin to take in the fresh air and calm her queasy stomach. It was early morning, and the sun was just starting to show itself above the horizon. As the sun climbed higher, it offered her a colorful display of bright pinks, yellows, and oranges. She continued to watch as the sun rose higher, and the bright colors gave way to a blue sky filled with white clouds.

"Could there have been a more beautiful morning?" asked Baxter. He wrapped his arms around her waist and kissed the top of her head. "It is mornings like this that make me glad that the Wispet Queen gave me the ability to walk in daylight."

"I always loved looking up at the night's sky, counting stars with my mother, and hoping to see a shooting star. If not for her gift, I would have missed the daylight too. I didn't realize how much until I watched the sunrise this morning. I have seen the sunrise nearly all of my life. It was something that happened every day. It brought color to my face and made me dread my woolen skirt on warm days. I never thought it was special. This morning, the sunrise was a gift that I will always treasure, and I am so grateful to the Wispet Queen for giving me the gift of walking in daylight."

Jario could hear them talking and cleared his throat as he stepped up to the railings next to Laralynn.

"I have had something on my mind that I have been unable to reconcile. I wonder if you might be able to help me?" asked Jario.

"If I can," replied Baxter.

"I went in search of Velsa and found her crumbled cottage. Later, I came upon her by accident as she tended her garden. She was at your old cottage, Laralynn, in Primrose Pond. I spoke to her, but she seemed afraid of me. What has happened to her?"

"To state it plainly and simply, she cut the tail from Lady Kayleigh's white wolf. For her crime, Lord Gautier, Desirae, Astra, Meadow, and the spirits of the dead witches, created a spell that took her magic and her memories away," replied Baxter. "She is human."

"She is known only by Aslev now," offered Laralynn.

"Velsa has paid dearly for her crime," replied Jario.

"It was time," Baxter said. "Anything else that troubles you?"

"There is something else," replied Jario. "I wanted to speak to you about the island and what to expect when we arrive. Like

Alabaster, your gifts will be useless."

"Has she spelled the island?" asked Laralynn.

"I believe she has, but I cannot be sure. A strange flickering light coming from the tower of her castle drew me to the island. Needing a place to hide from an army that I thought would chase me, I jumped from the ship and swam to its shore. It was then that I felt the heat."

"What heat?" asked Baxter.

"It comes from the sand and the air. Needing to find shelter, I made my way to the trees, but even there, I found no relief from the heat. It surrounds you, and there is no way to escape it."

Jario looked from Baxter to the white-capped waves as he remembered the darkness of the dungeon. Pushing it from his mind, he continued.

"I hadn't been on the island very long when I heard the sound of horses running toward me. I tried to pull my haze to hide, and that is when I realized my gifts were of no use to me. Her guards found me and took me to Firelight Castle. Once there, I was presented to Mistress Violeta."

"What is she like?"

Laralynn turned and leaned back against the railing wanting to hear more about her.

"She is beautiful but unusual. At our first meeting, her eyes were the color of amber, but the next time we met, they had changed to violet. Then, I noticed a violet light glowed where her heart should rest."

"How did you know where to find the sword?" asked Baxter. He had been suspicious of Jario's story from the beginning and surmised it was only a way to gain his freedom.

"I saw the sword hanging on the wall of Lord Gautier's hidden chamber. I touched it, heard the strange humming sound, and read the words engraved on the blade. It happened the day Lord Gautier and Lady Kayleigh were set free from the darkness of Velsa's spell. I had forgotten all about it until Mistress Violeta ordered me to bring it to her. I would have never returned to Alltree Island if it were not for her."

"I suppose you have more to gain than escaping your final death," laughed Laralynn. "Many others have told me of your greed."

"Mistress Violeta offered a reward for the sword's return," replied Jario. "It was not demanded by me. I will gladly accept what is offered, and never set my boots upon Alltree Island again."

"Land," yelled a man from the crow's nest.

"I think it best we get ready to meet the Firelight Army. They will be the first to welcome us to the Isle of Flames. I will warn you; they are intimidating," laughed Jario. "You might even find yourselves as unwelcome intruders and made to sleep on sour straw in the dungeon."

* * *

The *Withering Rose* dropped anchor near the Isle of Flames and lowered the boat that would take Jario, Baxter, and Laralynn to shore. With the sword strapped to Jario's back, he eagerly made his way down the knotted rope followed by Laralynn. After seeing her seated securely, he stood waiting for Baxter to descend the rope.

"Are you coming with us?" hollered Jario. "If you have changed your mind, it would be easy enough to leave you behind and send Laralynn back up to you."

"He's coming, Jario; he wanted words with the captain before he made his way down the rope," she grumbled.

"I assume he is begging him not to leave you behind if trouble should arise."

Looking up, he saw Baxter take to the rope. Annoyed, he sat down with a huff.

"Our bargain was to see me safely to the island. There was no need for an escort. I'm not a child."

"No, you are a traitor and a thief," smirked Baxter as he took his place beside Laralynn. "If I am to risk my position in the

Evergreen Army by giving you your freedom, I will make certain you are delivered to Mistress Violeta before I leave the island. What she does with you will no longer be my concern."

The boat began to move away from the ship and silence claimed its passengers until it nudged the soft sand of the island's shore. Jario jumped out and reached for Laralynn's hand. Refusing his help, she threw her legs over the side and stepped into the wet sand, letting the sea's foam circle her ankles. She immediately felt the warmth through the soft leather soles of her boots.

Feeling Baxter take her hand, they made their way toward the trees. Laralynn could feel the heat that Jario had described. The collar of her tunic was already damp, and she was glad she had taken a moment to pin her braids up off of her neck.

"This might be a good time to tell Baxter of the flames that covered your hands," sneered Jario. "You will be asked to state your gifts. She will know if you try to hide them from her."

Baxter looked at Laralynn with furrowed brows waiting for her to speak.

"I had forgotten all about it," she sighed. "It just happened when I was trying to keep the lions away from me."

"You were never given the gift by the Wispet Queen, which means, you gained it from my blood," he said, as his thoughts surmised the same might be true for him. He could see her start to smile, knowing she must have thought the same thing. He tried to enter her mind, not wanting to announce his suspicions for Jario to hear. The path was dark and closed off to him. He tried to flash back to the boat, but his boots held him securely on shore. His gifts were useless. "I tried to flash back to the boat. It is just as Jario said; our gifts are useless."

Jario looked toward the thick forest when he heard the thunder of hooves. He knew they would come for him, but this time, he wasn't worried. They were expecting him, and he would be treated with respect. After all, he brought Mistress Violeta the *Singing Sword*.

As quickly as the black stallions arrived, the guards

dismounted and stood glaring down at Baxter and Laralynn.

"Jario, why have you brought others with you?" barked the guardsman. "Your task was simple, bring our mistress the sword."

"There was need of a bargain to be made on my journey. The lieutenant needed my help to save the Lady Laralynn. I needed freedom from the Alabaster dungeon. In return for my help, he promised to free me from my cell and deliver me to the Mistress Violeta. It is nothing more than a promise kept," replied Jario. "However, I believe the Lady Lara of Evergreen Castle would be indebted to the mistress if a kindness would be shown to her daughter. You can see from her attire that she is in need of clothing befitting her station. I am sure the mistress would be hospitable in this regard."

"We'll see what the mistress has to say," replied the guardsman. "All of you, take to the horses. My Lady, you will ride with me."

Laralynn followed the guard to his stallion. He placed his hands around her waist and lifted her onto the stallion's back. As she reached for the black mane, she felt him settle in behind her. He took charge of the reins with one hand, and he placed his other hand gently around her waist.

"Forgive me, My Lady, the path is narrow and thick with low-hanging branches. I wish only to secure your person until we reach the castle."

"Your protection is willingly accepted," she replied.

The guard pulled on the reins and nudged the stallion with the heels of his boots. The stallion eagerly stomped his front hooves a few times, and then raced for the path that would take them all to Firelight Castle.

Chapter 21

Delivered

Laralynn found the ride through the forest fascinating. The leaves of every tree were either amber, red, or orange. She laughed when she realized the Isle of Flames was not a burning island as she had first thought. It merely gave the illusion of flames to keep unwanted visitors at bay. If it was magic, she thought it to be clever as well as beautiful.

As the trees thinned, Laralynn caught small glimpses of the castle through the branches. The stonework was gray, but it seemed to shimmer in the sunlight. A pleasant scent permeated the air, and she knew why when they broke through the trees. The castle was completely surrounded by wildflowers.

"It is beautiful," she cried. "I never expected anything like this."

"Our mistress finds it pleasing," the guardsman replied.

As they left the dirt path, the sound of the stallion's hooves clomping upon the smooth stones leading to the castle steps and its large wooden doors reminded her of home. Surprisingly, she found the sight comforting.

After reaching the stone steps, the guard dismounted and helped Laralynn to her feet. As the guards led the stallions away, she found Baxter coming toward her, and she reached for his hand. Hearing the groan of metal, they turned to see the wooden doors had opened, and a man had stepped out into the sunlight. He was tall with dark hair streaked with strands of white and tied at the nape of his neck. His tunic was white and cinched at the waist with a black leather sash. Over his heart sat a jeweled medallion bearing a black swan.

"On behalf of Mistress Violeta, I would like to welcome our new visitors to Firelight Castle. My name is Angus. Please, come with me."

Once inside, the guards escorted them to a chamber whose walls were lined with paintings, maps, and heads of animals mounted on plaques. Tall ornate cabinets stood on either side of the hearth that roared with dancing flames. Above the hearth, a silver shield held a single black swan. A long table stood at one end of the room filled with trays of bread spread with butter, meat, cheese, and pomegranates that revealed their juicy red seeds.

"This was not the welcome I received," muttered Jario. "I was hauled off to the dungeon and left there to rot."

"It appears she has had a change of heart," replied Laralynn. "I'm sure she will be pleased to see you have returned with the sword."

"Once you have done so, Laralynn and I will be on our way back to Evergreen," sighed Baxter. "I will be glad to get back to the Command Center. I've had enough of ships and ice."

"Let's hope the mistress lets you leave," smirked Jario.

Jario's words frightened Laralynn, but she tried not to show it. Without their gifts, they would be unable to leave the castle on their own. They would be guests of Mistress Violeta until she decided they could leave. It seemed they had traded Alabaster for the Isle of Flames.

With their bellies filled, they were each ushered off to private bedchambers to rest and wash the days of travel from their bodies. As Laralynn walked through the door, she was pleased to see the copper bathing tub filled with steaming water waiting for her. It had been too long since she had had the luxury of bathing in warm water.

A young woman closed the door behind her and softly said, "My Lady, my name is Francesca, but I prefer to be called Francey. I am to assist you with your bath and dressing you to meet the Mistress Violeta."

"Francey, my name is Laralynn. I would love for you to help me get these clothes off and take the pins from my hair. I can't wait to get into that tub of warm water and wash the grime from my body."

Laralynn sat while Francey pulled the pins from her hair, worked her tangled hair free of its braids, and pulled her dirty boots from her feet. With the dirty tunic and breeches clutched in Francey's arms, Laralynn made her way to the tub.

"Francey, throw those dirty things down and come help me wash my hair. It needs a good scrubbing, and I am longing to hear all about your mistress."

Laralynn stepped into the tub and sat down in the lavender scented water. A sea sponge floated on the water, and she eagerly pressed it to her forehead letting the water flow over her face.

"How long have you lived on the island?" asked Laralynn.

"I was born on the island," replied Francey as she poured a pitcher of water over Laralynn's hair. "My mother and father have a small cottage near Pollywog Pond. They make cheese for the castle."

"We have something in common, Francey. I grew up in a small cottage with my mother in Primrose Pond. We had a very naughty goat, and I helped my mother make cheese to sell at Ian's Market."

"We do have things in common," replied Francey.

"How did you come to work at the castle?" asked Laralynn.

"My father sold my services to Mistress Violeta."

"He sold you?"

"It is not what you think. The mistress has given me a tutor, and I am learning to speak different languages, to read, and the makings of numbers. The mistress hopes to take me with her when she is free to leave the island."

"I see, he has cleverly given you a wonderful gift."

"It is one that I will always treasure. Now, close your eyes, My Lady, while I pour soap upon your hair. I have found that it stings the eyes."

Francey washed and rinsed Laralynn's hair while answering all of her questions about the island, the castle, and her mistress. Once her hair was rinsed clean, she helped Laralynn out of the tub and wrapped her in a robe. While they sat by the fire and talked, Francey brushed Laralynn's hair until it was dry and then wove ribbons through the loose braid that hung down her back.

"Are you ready to choose a gown? Come, we need to get you dressed. Angus will be calling for you soon." Francey opened the armoire doors and ran her hand across the skirts of three gowns. "There is a blue one, a green one, and a coral one. Which do you like best?"

"I'll wear the green gown. It reminds me of the forest near my home."

Francey pulled the gown from the armoire and laid it across the bed. She opened a trunk and carefully removed an under-slip, corset, and stockings.

Francey had just tied the ribbons of Laralynn's slippers when they heard a knock at the door.

"Lady Laralynn, it is time," called Angus.

* * *

Laralynn held tightly to Angus' arm as they descended the stone steps. She felt uneasy on her feet and feared she might tumble to the floor. There had been no worries in the bedchamber, but now her limbs trembled with every step. Angus must have known of her uneasiness, for he patted her hand several times to reassure her. He had even offered to carry her down the steps.

Finally reaching the bottom, she offered Angus a smile and whispered, "Angus, I thank you for your arm. Had it not been for you, I would have surely fallen and landed with my skirt above my head. I would have been a sight for all to see."

Angus laughed, replying, "Then let's be glad your skirt is long and still brushing the tops of your toes."

As they entered the hall, Laralynn could see Jario and Baxter standing before an empty throne. She wanted to run to Baxter's side, but Angus kept a firm grip on her arm as they slowly made their way to his side.

"I will leave you here beside your friend," he said, as he released her arm. "Mistress Violeta will be here soon."

He bowed his head and quickly took to the steps toward a narrow door.

"You look lovely," offered Baxter. "It has been a while since I have seen you in something other than breeches."

"You look very handsome, yourself," she replied. "I see you were rewarded with a bath too. Wasn't it glorious?"

"It was indeed."

Jario stood balancing the tip of the sword on the toe of his boot trying to ignore their whispering. He would be glad when they left the island, and he could get on with his new life.

There was a single rap on the door, and Angus pulled the door open. Four men walked through the open doorway and took their place before their thrones. Laralynn saw Angus draw his fist to his chest and then a woman walked into the chamber. She was beautiful, just as Jario had said. Her raven colored hair was pulled back from her face and held in place by combs adorned with large silver-gray pearls. The neckline of her silver gown was low enough to reveal a black swan pendant covered in pearls that hung around her neck. She stood for a moment in front of her throne eyeing the sword and then sat down. The four men followed her lead.

"Welcome to my home; I am Violeta. I know the vampire, Jario, but I don't believe that I have seen either of you on the island. Your names, please."

Laralynn took a step forward and made a deep curtsy, "My name is Laralynn Evergreen. I am the daughter of Lord Thomas and Lady Lara of Evergreen Castle."

"I know of your home and the lords yearning for peace," replied Violeta. "And, the young man that stands beside you?"

Baxter stepped next to Laralynn and bowed his head. "I am Lt. Baxter Marsh of the Evergreen Army and Guardian of the Lady Laralynn."

"I believe you to be more than her guardian," she laughed. "Have you been Jario's guardian, as well?"

"I was ordered to bring him to Evergreen Castle, but we ran into some trouble along the way. I needed his help, and he informed me of his need to deliver you a sword. We made a bargain. He honored his promise, and in return, I have honored my promise and brought him here."

"It is good that you did, for he would have paid dearly had he not returned with the sword," replied Violeta. "Jario, I see the sword you have brought me. I would like to examine it."

She watched him carry the sword across the palms of his hands. Her eagerness caused her to meet him half way. As she looked down at the blade, a gasp passed from her lips when she saw the engraving, *Fuaim na Cumhacta*. Running her finger over the words, she heard the sweet humming sound and felt the start of a tear. Turning quickly, she looked up at Angus.

"Angus, retrieve the sword. He has fulfilled his task." She turned and faced the four men that sat quietly on their thrones. "This is the *Singing Sword*, and I claim it as my own."

Angus made his way down the steps and retrieved the sword from Jario.

"Take it to my bedchamber and lay it across the foot of my bed."

He nodded and left her side making his way through the narrow doorway.

"You have made me very happy, Jario," she said. "To show my thanks, there will be a celebration feast tomorrow evening in your honor."

"Thank you, Mistress Violeta," he replied.

"Until then, I will leave you to dine without me this evening. The excitement of receiving the sword has exhausted me.

Forgive me, but I must retire to my bedchamber."

She lifted the hem of her gown and made her way up the steps. Turning to look at Jario one more time, she saw him offer her a smile and then hurried off to her bedchamber.

Chapter 22

Released

Alight tapping woke Laralynn from her dreams. As she sat up clutching the bed linens to her breast, she heard the tapping again. Someone was at her door. Slipping from her bed, she tiptoed across the cold floor and put her ear to the door.

"Who is there?" she whispered.

"It is Violeta. May I come in?"

Laralynn unlatched and opened the door. Mistress Violeta quickly entered and closed the door behind her.

"It is time for you and your guardian to leave the island. I have come to help you dress and take you to the guards."

"I don't understand. How are we to find our way through the dark forest? Would it not be better to leave in the light of day?"

"No, we must leave before morning light. The ship is eager to sail."

"You said, we. Are you coming with us?"

"Yes, I am coming with you. I have longed for this day, and I can wait no longer. I will explain, but you need to get dressed. Angus has gone to wake your guardian. They will meet us outside on the stone steps. The horses have been readied, and the guards stand ready to take us to the shore."

As Violeta took clothes from the chest, Laralynn pulled her

gown over her head. Standing naked and cold, she accepted the shift she was given and pulled it over her head. Violeta pulled a woolen skirt from the bottom of the chest and tossed it on the bed. Laralynn quickly grabbed it, found the sash, and began tying it around her waist. Violeta gasped when the door opened, and Francey walked in carrying a sack.

"They are all waiting for you. I thought you might need some help," smiled Francey.

She dropped her sack on the floor and went to the armoire. After opening the doors, she removed soft leather boots and tossed them to Laralynn. As quickly as she could, she pulled everything else to the floor and began stuffing it in her sack.

"Francey, I'd prefer my breeches over the gowns you are packing," laughed Laralynn.

"They aren't for you," replied Francey. They're for me. Now, fasten that skirt and slip on those boots." She pulled a shawl from the pile and tossed it at Laralynn's feet. "You might need this to wrap around your shoulders once we are on the ship."

Violeta walked to the door carrying a sack filled with clothes and stood nervously tapping her foot.

"Had you told me about this earlier, I could have been ready when you tapped on my door," fussed Laralynn as she flung the shawl over her shoulders. "Lead the way, but don't leave me behind."

Violeta put her finger to her lips and opened the door. Finding no one lingering in the hallway, she held tight to her sack and hurried toward the stone steps with Laralynn and Francey close behind.

* * *

Baxter was already seated behind a guard when Laralynn stepped out into the night air. Angus held Francey's sack while a guard pulled her up to settle herself in front of him. The same guardsman that had carried Laralynn to the castle stood waiting to help her mount his stallion. Violeta stood before Angus with tears in her eyes as she said her final good-bye. He kissed the top of her head and turned her toward a waiting guard.

"Wait, my sword?" she asked.

"It is secured to your guard's back."

"Thank you, Angus, for everything."

"It was my pleasure, mistress. Go, it is time. There is nothing left for you here."

All at once, the guards nudged their stallions with the heels of their boots. One after another, they raced for the forest. Angus stood on the stone steps until he could no longer see her. He removed the medallion from his chest and entered the castle, closing the doors behind him.

The ride through the forest brought the same heat to their faces as when they arrived, but a strange sight caused her to lean back against the guard. The leaves were glowing.

"Why do the leaves glow?" asked Laralynn. "Will they hurt us?"

"They are saying goodbye to their mistress," he replied.

Reaching the shore, they found a guard with a lantern standing near the water and a boat heading toward the shore. Everyone quickly dismounted, and Baxter helped Francey with the sacks. The guards stood in a line waiting for their mistress. As she approached, they knelt before her. She placed her hand upon their heads and whispered a farewell message in their ears. The last guard held the sword out to her, and Laralynn watched as her trembling hands drew it tightly to her chest.

"The boat has arrived, mistress. It is time to leave," said the guard.

Baxter helped Francey and Laralynn into the boat. He held out his hand to Violeta and waited for her to step forward.

"What if it won't let me leave?" she cried.

"But, what if it does?" replied Baxter.

Violeta smiled and took Baxter's hand. He lifted her up and carried her to the boat. Once he saw her seated, he climbed in after her and took his place next to Laralynn.

"Take me to the *Withering Rose*, kind sir. My freedom awaits," ordered Violeta.

She could feel every stroke of the oars that swept through the water. With every stroke, it tore away the curse that had bound her to the island. She finally had the sword she had longed for and the freedom the wizard had stolen from her. Once they were all on deck, the captain waved his lantern and the guard on the island did the same, in return. She watched the fading light in the lantern go dark and turned her back on the island.

"Let's get you to your cabin," offered the captain.

Violeta suddenly felt a prickling heat coming from the blade of the sword. The heat began to burn her hands, and she dropped the sword at her feet. Seeing the sword turn a bright red, Baxter pulled her back to keep her safe.

"No, don't send me back to the island. I have my freedom," Violeta cried.

The sound of someone singing filled the air as an iridescent mist seeped from the blade forming a cloud. It grew larger and moved toward Violeta. She gasped when she felt someone reach for her hand and whisper her name.

"Who is there? What do you want from me?" she cried, fearing the wizard had returned to send her back to the island.

The cloud began to fade and in its place stood a tall handsome man with broad shoulders and brown hair tied at the nape of his neck. His eyes were hazel, and they held Violeta's bewildered stare.

"Ewan?"

"I have waited so long to hear you say my name. Please, let me hear you say it again."

"Oh, Ewan!" She threw her arms around his waist and pressed her face against his chest. His heartbeat was strong. Remembering the violet light that covered her heart, she backed away and looked down to find it had disappeared.

"Your sword, it's gone," gasped Francey. "It has vanished."

"The Wizard Jessop cursed me to live within the sword. Now that I'm free, the sword no longer exists. We are free, my love. We are finally free of the curse."

Chapter 23

Promises

There had been too much excitement for anyone to desire sleep. Instead, they sat on the deck listening to Violeta and Ewan tell their stories. Someone asked what happened to her father, and Violeta just shrugged her shoulders. Laralynn knew she had no way of knowing about her father's disastrous end. She had already been cursed to the island when he died. It was not her tale to tell. Violeta would hear of it one day, but not on a night filled with happiness.

Francey was the first to yawn and wander off to her cabin. It wasn't long before the crew and captain left for their beds. Seeing Violeta had fallen asleep in Ewan's arms, Baxter reached for Laralynn's hand and helped her stand.

"Before you go, I must apologize for the illness that I brought upon the Lady Laralynn," whispered Ewan.

"I don't understand, what illness?" asked Laralynn.

"Even though the Wizard Jessop cursed me to the sword, I could hear everything around me. It was like I was a helpless blind man. I was unable to speak or move. I was traded and sold, hung on walls, hidden under beds, and stored in a dark chamber. You can't imagine the things that I have heard over the years. I heard tears of joy and sadness, the sounds of war, frightening curses, and cries for help. I could barely contain my excitement the day that Jario stole me. I knew that Violeta charged Jario with returning the sword to her. He talked to himself, constantly. It made my head hurt, and I found that I longed for the silence," Ewan quietly laughed before he continued. "If you recall, the day you found Jario hiding upon the ice there was a struggle. Laralynn, you claimed the sword. I was afraid that you would return it to the darkness of that hidden chamber, and I would be lost to Violeta forever. I made you ill in hopes that you would return it to Jario. In doing so, it kept you from returning safely to Evergreen. I am to blame for your fall through the ice and everything that followed. I am truly sorry."

"I knew of Violeta's need for the sword. It was told to us by the witch, Meadow, at the council meeting. You had no way of knowing our plan. Do not think of it anymore. Ewan, you are forgiven," replied Laralynn. "We are both happy that you are free."

"Let's get you to your cabin. It has been a long evening," whispered Baxter to Laralynn.

She nodded to Ewan, and they quietly made their way to Laralynn's cabin door.

"Will you sit with me?" she asked. "I need to talk."

He nodded and followed her into her cabin. Laralynn pulled off her boots and climbed onto the small bed.

"Come sit on the bed. It's more comfortable than that stool."

He pulled off his boots and climbed onto the bed. Sitting cross-legged, he asked, "What's bothering you?"

"Why was Jario left on the island? I'm worried about the people that live there."

"Angus told me Violeta promised him a castle, wealth, and power if he brought her the sword."

"That doesn't answer my question. We all left under the cover of darkness, and Jario knew nothing of it. Doesn't that seem strange to you?"

"Laralynn, I promised to take him safely to the island so that he might return the *Singing Sword* to Mistress Violeta, and this is where I will leave him. It is up to him to make his own way, and I will not interfere unless he finds his way back to Alltree Island. You should be happy for Violeta. That sword was her only way off the island. We helped Jario, and in return, he helped her break the curse. In doing so, she has been reunited with Ewan."

"What of the people? Francey's mother and father live on the island. They make cheese for the castle. What will happen to them if Jario reverts to his evil ways?"

"Angus is there to watch over the castle. He promised he would keep the people safe."

"What can Angus do to protect the people from an evil vampire?"

"Angus is the reason we all lost our gifts when we stepped on the warm sand. He spelled the sand to take away a vampire's gifts. They won't return unless he leaves the island."

"Angus is a wizard?"

"Yes, he is a wizard, and he has promised to warn us if Jario ever leaves the island."

"Jario is lucky to have found Firelight Castle and Angus. If you had taken him back to Evergreen, my mother would have given him his final death. At least he will never bother anyone on Alltree Island again."

Laralynn brought her hand to her mouth and yawned. Baxter knew she was tired, but he wasn't ready to leave her yet. He slid off the bed and pulled on his boots.

"Laralynn put on your boots and come with me."

"Where?"

"The sky is clear tonight. Come watch the stars with me. We haven't looked up at the stars for such a long time."

Laralynn offered him a smile, and he had his answer. He helped her with her boots and led her up the stairs toward the stern of the ship. The crew that remained on duty stood on the quarterdeck, and he wanted to be completely alone with the woman that had stolen his heart.

They leaned against the railing and stared up at the night's sky covered with stars. It wasn't long before Laralynn saw a shooting star and pointed to the sky.

"Baxter, make a wish before it's gone."

They held hands and both made a wish.

"What did you wish?" he asked.

"I wished we would be home soon, and everyone would be happy to see us. What did you wish?"

"I wished that we could be together for all eternity."

Suddenly, Baxter turned to face Laralynn and knelt on one knee.

"Laralynn, I have known for a very long time that you were the only one that would make my life complete. If you will have me, I promise to care for you, protect you, and love you above all others. Will you do me the honor of becoming my mate for all eternity?"

Kneeling before him, she cupped his face with her hands and looked into his eyes. "I love you, Baxter, above all others, and I will be honored to become your mate for all eternity."

Baxter opened his pouch and withdrew a gold ring engraved with apple blossoms. Nestled in the center of each delicate flower was an emerald that sparkled in the moonlight. He took her hand and gently slipped it on her finger. Turning her hand over, he leaned down and kissed her palm.

"You have made me so very happy," he whispered.

"It is beautiful, Baxter," she replied, as she wrapped her arms around him. "I will treasure it and our love, always."

* * *

Laralynn woke to the gentle touch of Francey's hand upon her shoulder. Sitting up, she wiped the sleep from her eyes and inhaled the sweet aroma of honey swirled in clover tea.

"My Lady, there is a buzz about the ship this morning. Your little secret is a secret no longer," laughed Francey.

"What little secret?" asked Laralynn.

"Mr. Feathers, the man that sits in the crow's nest, saw

Baxter kneeling at your feet last night. Your sweet embrace told him of your answer. He has been singing the news all morning."

"It was a glorious night, Francey. It was so romantic. I am so very happy."

The cabin door opened and Violeta walked in with a coral gown embroidered with gold flowers draped over her arm. She held a pair of matching slippers from their ribbons in one hand and a strand of pearls in the other.

"Let's get you dressed. The sky is just the perfect shade for a morning wedding," coaxed Violeta as she handed the gown to Francey.

"Who's wedding?" yawned Laralynn taking the cup of tea from Violeta's hand.

"Baxter asked the captain if he had ever performed a marriage ceremony on his ship. He said he had not, but he would love to do the honor someday. Then, Baxter asked if he would perform your marriage ceremony this morning."

"Our what?" choked Laralynn. "Here . . . This morning . . . On this ship?"

"Yes! Dear Laralynn, it is your wedding day," shrieked Francey. "Now, let's get you ready before he thinks you have changed your mind."

Francey had curled and decorated her hair with ribbons she had taken from the castle. Violeta had tugged, cinched, squeezed, and even pinched her before she was finally dressed. After stepping into her matching coral slippers and Francey tying the ribbons about her ankles, Violeta hung the strand of pearls around her neck.

"You look beautiful," Violeta sighed. "Now, let's take you to Baxter."

Standing on the quarterdeck, she felt Ewan take her hand and guide her down the steps. She could see Baxter standing in front of the captain, and her knees felt weak. Resting her hand on Ewan's arm, she slowly made her way towards Baxter's side.

As Laralynn offered her hand to Baxter, she took in the pink and coral hues that painted the early morning sky. She glanced over at the man that had loved her, protected her, and saved her. She listened to the simple vows of love they spoke, and they brought tears to her eyes. It had been a ceremony filled with beauty and love, and she would always remember it.

As the captain said the final words that united them as one, the sound of a cannon's blast celebrated their union. Baxter gently lifted Laralynn's chin and sealed their vows with a kiss as everyone cheered their names.

"Did you like your surprise?" smiled Baxter. "I couldn't wait any longer."

"It was a lovely surprise. Now, it is my turn to surprise you."

She wrapped her arms around his waist, and they vanished.

* * *

Jario woke to the sound of servants moving about his bedchamber. He watched as they busied themselves with drawing back the velvet window coverings, tending the hearth, filling his bathing tub, and laying out his clothes. He heard a soft rap on the door before another servant entered carrying a tray piled high with bread, fruit, cheese, and a goblet of what he knew to be blood.

I've missed this luxurious attention, he thought.

Slipping from his bed and donning his robe of red brocade trimmed in fur, he made his way to the small table and lifted the goblet to breathe in the intoxicating scent. Pressing the rim of the goblet to his lips, he raised it slowly letting the wonderfully rich liquid caress his tongue as it flowed down his throat. It was definitely not animal blood, but the taste was unlike anything he had ever tasted. It was pure ambrosia.

As he placed the empty goblet back on the table, he saw a folded parchment sealed with red wax embedded with a small black swan. Turning it over in his hand, he found his name beautifully written in large letters.

"It must be an invitation to the celebration the Mistress Violeta has planned for me," he announced, for the servants to hear. He eagerly broke the seal, unfolded the parchment, and began to read.

LET IT BE KNOWN
TO ALL THAT DWELL ON THE ISLE OF FLAMES
FROM THIS DAY AND FOR ALL ETERNITY
I, MISTRESS VIOLETA
BESTOW TO JARIO
FIRELIGHT CASTLE
AND
ALL ITS WEALTH AND POWER

Jario looked up to find Angus had entered the bedchamber.

"She has given me Firelight Castle," Jario informed Angus. "Why? I don't understand."

"Did she not promise you a great reward for bringing her the *Singing Sword*?" replied Angus.

"I did not expect her to give up her castle. Her generosity is overwhelming."

"You may not think her generous when you hear the whole story."

"What story?"

"Mistress Violeta was cursed to live on this island until someone brought her the *Singing Sword*. It was the only thing that would set her free."

"Has she gone?"

"Yes, she has gone from the island, and you have taken her place."

"What does that mean? I have taken her place?"

"The Wizard Jessop's curse has been passed to you. You are the new Master of Firelight Castle. As it was with Mistress Violeta, it is the same for you. The *Singing Sword* is your only hope for freedom from this island."

While those words were playing over and over in Jario's mind, Angus quietly left the bedchamber.

The parchment fell from his hand and drifted to the floor as Jario made his way toward the open doors leading to the balcony. He longed to feel a cool breeze against his face, but the warmth of the morning sun was all that greeted him. Leaning against the stone railing, he felt the weight of something brush against his chest. Reaching inside his robe, his hand touched a familiar object. It was the medallion Mistress Violeta had given him. He tore it from his neck and smashed it against the stone railing. Furious, his eyes scanned the horizon. He could see the *Withering Rose* as it sailed away carrying the woman that had betrayed him.

"I'll send someone to bring me the *Singing Sword*. You'll not make me a prisoner on the Isle of Flames for long!" he shouted.

As he turned his back on the *Withering Rose*, he heard the blast of a cannon and felt his chest burn from within. Looking down, he saw the glow of a violet light against his skin and dropped to his knees.

* * *

Little did Jario know that the *Singing Sword* no longer existed. As the new Master of Firelight Castle, he has been bound to the Isle of Flames as a powerless vampire, and his fate has been sealed forever.

Will it be a fate worse than his final death?

Only time will tell.

Epilogue

Rays of the morning sun were beginning to spill upon the floor of their bedchamber when Baxter woke to the sound of Laralynn crying. He gently pulled her against his chest and wrapped his arms around her.

"Wake, my love," he whispered, as he inhaled her scent of fresh apples. "It is only a bad dream and nothing to fear."

She wiped the sleep from her eyes and snuggled closer, relishing the comfort of his voice and his loving embrace.

"Laralynn, I have you, and nothing can harm you."

"We will protect each other, won't we, Baxter?"

"Always," he replied, as he kissed the top of her head. "Now, tell me about your dream, and I'll try to make it go away."

"I was standing in the meadow just beyond Evergreen Forest picking wildflowers, and I could see Astra coming toward me. Suddenly, she was covered with beautiful red butterflies. She fell to the ground, and I could hear her cries for help. I tried to run toward her, but my feet were sinking into the ground. I couldn't help her."

He could feel her body tremble, and he pulled the coverlet up over her bare arms.

"It was just a dream; there is no need to worry."

"Do you think my dream might have some special meaning? After all, I dreamt of a faceless man coming for my magical sword, and it came true. Jario came to our island and stole the

Singing Sword from Black Thistle Castle."

"It was merely a coincidence, Laralynn."

"Was it really a coincidence or something more?"

"If it worries you speak to Meadow. She has visions of things to come."

"I will do as you suggest. I shall seek Meadow's advice today. She will know if it was a vision or only a dream."

"For now, try not to think about your bad dreams. Think about something else and push the worry out of your mind. This is our time to enjoy each other."

"What shall I think of?"

"Think about the morning we wed, our first night together, and how much I love you."

"And, how happy we will be for all eternity?"

"Yes, how happy we will be for all eternity."

She turned within his embrace and looked up into his eyes.

"I love you, Baxter, with all my heart."

"I love you, too, my lavender eyed beauty," he whispered.

"Now, let me show you how much."

The End

A Note From The Author

Thank you for reading Laralynn's TURN. I loved writing about Laralynn's journey to Alabaster, and I was thrilled to finally give Jario the justice he deserved. Even though he didn't receive his final death, I believe thinking about his failures for eternity is much sweeter.

If you enjoyed this book, it would mean so much to me if you would please take a moment to leave a review on Amazon, Goodreads, or your favorite provider. Every review, long or short, is important to an author.

What's coming next? I am currently working on another Evergreen Novel, Revenge - On Poison Wings. Gisela, a new character, will journey to Alltree Island seeking revenge for her son's death. Astra is her target, and Oliver will do all he can to protect her.

I would love to hear from my readers. Let me know what you think of the characters in the Evergreen Novels and who you would like to hear more about. You can reach me at any of the sites below. I will do my best to respond as quickly as I can. I look forward to hearing from you.

Website: www.authorjoannherley.com

Facebook: www.facebook.com/authorjhbooks

Email: info@authorjoannherley.com

www.ingramcontent.com/pod-product-compliance
Lightning Source LLC
Chambersburg PA
CBHW061231170626
46809CB00007B/2614

* 9 7 8 0 6 9 2 8 7 9 1 8 4 *